Grasping Toby's wrist with surprising strength, she steered him toward the escalator, without apologizing to the clerk for all his needless trouble. Toby looked wretchedly back toward his real mother—but she appeared not to have seen him; she was deep in conversation with that other boy. Perhaps she was not his mother at all? Who *am* I? Toby wondered. If I'm not her son, do I have to go with this woman? He did not want to in the least—he felt a strong, instinctive dislike for her. But what else could he do? Where could he go?

QUANTITY SALES

Most Dell books are available at special quantity discounts when purchased in bulk by corporations, organizations, and special-interest groups. Custom imprinting or excerpting can also be done to fit special needs. For details write: Dell Publishing, 666 Fifth Avenue, New York, NY 10103. Attn.: Special Sales Department.

INDIVIDUAL SALES

Are there any Dell books you want but cannot find in your local stores? If so, you can order them directly from us. You can get any Dell book in print. Simply include the book's title, author, and ISBN number if you have it, along with a check or money order (no cash can be accepted) for the full retail price plus $2.00 to cover shipping and handling. Mail to: Dell Readers Service, P.O. Box 5057, Des Plaines, IL 60017.

A Touch of Chill

TALES FOR SLEEPLESS NIGHTS

Joan Aiken

Published by
Dell Publishing
a division of
Bantam Doubleday Dell Publishing Group, Inc.
666 Fifth Avenue
New York, New York 10103

Some of the stories in this book were first published in Great Britain as follows:

"A Game of Black and White," " 'He,' " "Listening," "Lodgers," "The Sewanee Glide," "Time to Laugh," and "Who Goes Down This Dark Road?" in *A Touch of Chill* (Gollancz, 1979); "Power-Cut" in *A Book of Contemporary Nightmares* (Michael Joseph, 1977); "Elephant's Ear," "Mousework," and "Sailors' Legends" in *Windscreen Weepers* (Gollancz, 1969) and in *Argosy* (1960, 1961); and "The Cat Flap and the Apple Pie" in *The Cat Flap and the Apple Pie and Other Funny Stories* (W. J. Allen, 1979).

ISBN: 0-440-20459-3

RL: 8.0

Reprinted by arrangement with Delacorte Press

Printed in the United States of America

October 1989

10 9 8 7 6 5 4 3 2 1

KRI

Contents

The Cat Flap and the Apple Pie

It was the last day of summer vacation. Apples lay about all over the grass. A burnt patch on the lawn showed where the boys had had a bonfire, the week before, and cooked sausages. Wet, sandy swimming trunks hung on the clothesline, and several dozen seashells were strewn over the front path, where somebody had dropped them and somebody else had kicked them.

The Crask family was having breakfast. Tim Crask had already eaten his and was cramming bread and cheese into his jacket pockets.

"I'm going down to Beezeley's farm to drive the tractor," he said. "Shan't be back till suppertime."

"It's illegal to drive a tractor at your age," said Mr. Crask, with his head in the newspaper. He had been saying this all through the summer.

"I'm driving it in a field, not on the road," said Tim as he had all through the summer.

"Mind you get back in time to put your things together for school," said Mrs. Crask. "Have you done your vacation work?"

Tim took no notice of this.

"There's a horrible draft coming from the back door," said Mr. Crask. "Can somebody shut it?"

"Mishkin's outside."

"For heaven's sake! Can't that kitten learn to meow, if he wants to come in?"

"Nobody hears him. And that big fat black tom of the Kingsleys' chases him—he hasn't got *time* to meow."

"Well, leave the pantry window open."

"Then the Kingsleys' cat comes in and beats him up in here."

"I wish we'd never *got* that cat," Mr. Crask said from inside his paper.

The phone rang.

"Answer it, will you, Tim, there's a love, as you're standing up," said Mrs. Crask, who was washing twenty jampots preparatory to making blackberry and apple jelly.

Tim scowled but answered the phone, which was in the hall.

"It's Aunt Daphne, wanting to speak to Dad," he said, returning with an expressionless face.

Mr. Crask went into the hall.

"Hello, Daphne," they heard him say. "Oh—are you? Yes, that would be perfectly okay. No, we aren't—good to see you all. What time will you get here? Yes, yes, we're all here—school starts tomorrow. Fine—see you, then."

Mr. Crask's telephone conversations never lasted long. He came back into the kitchen, having hardly stopped reading his paper, which he carried with him, and sat down again.

"Daphne and Bob and the girls are coming to lunch," he announced, looking over the top for a moment.

"*What?*" shrieked his wife.

George's face assumed an expression of settled despair. Tim walked quietly out of the house, mounted his bike, and rode off.

"*Tim!* Come back!"

No good. Tim was already out of earshot.

"You *asked* them to *lunch*—when you know I've got all the boys' school clothes to go through—and I was going to make blackberry jelly—"

"They asked themselves. They said they were driving by this way. What else could I do?"

"*I* won't talk to those horrible girls," George said. "All they can do is brag about their school and how well they did in their exams."

"You certainly *will* talk to them," said his father. "It's very rude not to. What will you give them for lunch, Ann?"

Mrs. Crask looked distraught.

"George, do you think you could cycle down to the butcher and get some beef cubes? Then I suppose I could make a stew."

"Stew! That's not very festive."

"I don't feel very festive," said Mrs. Crask flatly.

"Yes, I'll go," said George, who liked stew. "Then I can get a cat flap at Moxon's, and put in the back door."

"*I'm* not paying for any cat flap," said Mr. Crask.

"I've got enough money myself. From potato-picking," said George.

"Well, don't come running to *me* when you've made a mess of it," said his father. George didn't answer that one.

Breakfast was over. Mr. Crask strolled out to finish reading his paper in the garden, as the weather was so fine and warm. Mrs. Crask looked around the house, which was a total mess. A lot of leftover picnic things had been dumped in the hall. The dining room had been used for a game of Progressive Ping-Pong, with obstacles piled up around the table to make it harder for the players to run from one end to the other. The living room had a lot of deck chairs in it because it had begun to rain suddenly last night, and it was quicker to bring the chairs in than to take them all the way down to the shed.

"We'll have to straighten the house," Mrs. Crask said to George when he came back with the meat and the cat flap.

"I want to fix this in the back door. Look," said George, as Mishkin, the marmalade kitten, shot across the lawn, pursued by the fat black tom from next door. George rushed out and aimed a swipe at the black tom with a baseball bat but missed him and chopped the heads off a clump of marigolds. Mishkin came indoors wailing and wanting to be picked up and petted. One of his ears was covered with blood. George took the cat flap out of its wrappings.

"Straighten the house *first*, before you start on the cat flap," his mother said.

George gloomily helped her.

"It's unfair that Tim gets out of this," he said.

It was unfair, and his mother knew it.

"Life is unfair," she said. "It's unfair that I have to make lunch for the Bewdleys when I want to get on with my jam."

"I *hate* those girls," said George. "Susan wears lipstick. *Lipstick!* Ugh."

"What are you going to give them for dessert?" Mr. Crask shouted from the front garden.

"They can have bread and cheese and fruit, as we've done all summer."

"They most certainly can *not*! Why don't you make them an apple pie? Daphne loves your orange-flavored apple pies. Yes," said Mr. Crask, "make them an apple pie."

"Oh, *fudge*," muttered Mrs. Crask.

Dashing about, she and George straightened the dining room and the living room, hurling everything into the closet under the stairs. The stew was begun and put on to simmer. George scrubbed a lot of potatoes, ready for baking.

Then he got a fretsaw and cut an oblong out of the back door, the same size as the cat flap that he had bought. The job was hideously difficult, because the back door was made of hard, weathered boards, very likely fifty years old. Also, his mother kept interrupting him.

"George, could you go and pick me some parsley and thyme. George, could you be a love and take this basket and get some string beans, enough for seven people."

"It's like eating baseball bats," grumbled George, returning with the basket of enormous, tough, stringy beans. As he shut the back door, the fat black tom from the next house jumped in through the hole he had just sawed. *"Get out!"* said George, furiously swatting it with the basket. Beans flew about the kitchen.

Mrs. Crask let out a sudden shriek.

"Now what's the matter, Mom?"

"I put the orange for the apple pie into the oven to soften up and forgot all about it. Now it's gone all brown and hard."

"Pour boiling water on it," suggested George, looking at the pie dish of cut-up orange pieces; they had turned mahogany brown.

"But that would dilute the orange flavor," objected his mother.

"Pour on some orange soda then."

"No—I know—I'll soak them in sherry."

"That's not orange flavor."

"No, but it's fairly like. And doesn't taste so phony as orange soda. And then I'll put them back in the oven, just for a minute or two, to soften up again. *Don't let me forget they're in the oven.* Oh, George, could you be an *angel* and go and pick up some windfall apples. Enough to make a pie."

While George was picking up the apples, the phone rang.

"Could you answer it, Andrew," called Mrs. Crask to her husband. "My hands are all covered in pastry."

"Never get a *minute* to read the *paper,"* grumbled Mr. Crask, coming into the hall. He snatched up the receiver. "Yes, who is it? Oh, Daphne, you again—What is it now?"

George, returning with the apples, met his mother's eyes.

"Perhaps they can't come after all," she whispered hopefully.

"Oh, Andrew dear," said his sister at the other end, "look, it seems the girls invited their friend Felicity for the day. Will it be all right if we bring her along too?"

"Oh, sure. Two or three, four or five, what's the difference?" said Mr. Crask heartily. "See you then. 'Bye."

"The girls are bringing that friend of theirs too," he shouted through the kitchen door. "Lord, this room's a mess! I hope you straighten it up before they come."

He returned to his paper.

"Oh, *not* that *awful Felicity!*" said George, aghast. "I cannot *stand* it! Well, I'm certainly not going to talk to *her.*"

"George, you must. I'm sorry, but you must. Oh *damn*— my bits of orange!"

Mrs. Crask leapt to the oven.

The orange pulp had now cooked to a dark brown goo, but the slices of peel were still as tough as oak bark.

"If *I* were you, I should just use the goo and throw away the peel," said George.

"There won't be enough goo to flavor the pie, without the peel."

"Well, mash it all up with the little mixer then. I'll do that if you like," said George, who was rather fond of using the little mixer. It was a single electric prong with a tiny fierce windmill at its tip; you had to be very careful when using it, for if the windmill part came above the surface of whatever you were mixing, splashes shot all over the room.

Indeed, it proved to be a mistake to use it on the baked cut-up orange. The blades of the windmill kept encountering hard bits of orange peel, and the kitchen was soon generously spattered with dark brown gooey splashes.

"Stop, *stop!*" shouted Mrs. Crask. "You are wasting all my orange on the walls."

"Well, you'd better put it in the big blender then," advised George.

"There's hardly any left," said Mrs. Crask, looking into the bottom of the dish.

"Add some more sherry to it."

Even so, Mrs. Crask had to keep tilting the big blender from side to side, or the blades went round uselessly, without finding anything to mince up.

"All this for an apple pie for those brutes to eat!" said George, and he went back to work on his cat flap. The flap came in two parts, a frame, which fitted into the hole he had cut, and a hinged door, which slotted into the frame. At this point George realized that he had put the frame in upside down. While he was reversing it, the fat black tom from next door chased Mishkin through the hole. Mishkin fled screaming and knocked over the pot of glue that George had been using. George grabbed a ratchet screwdriver and aimed a swipe at the black tom, just missing him. As he had picked up the screwdriver by the blade part, he cut his hand quite deeply, but did not notice this until he began to wonder where all the blood on the floor was coming from.

Mishkin sat up on top of the broom closet, wailing.

The phone rang again.

"Someone *else* will have to get it *this* time," said Mr. Crask. "I'm just going for some cigarettes. *Good god,* what a mess," he said, looking at the floor inside the back door, which was covered with glue, sawdust, wood splinters, blood, and tools. "I hope you'll have the kindness to get that cleared up before they come."

George answered the phone, covering the receiver with blood and glue.

"Oh, hello, Aunt Daphne. Yes. I see. You want to get here at twelve, for an early lunch, because the girls want to go to the beach afterwards. Yes. Okay. Good-bye," said George tonelessly, and he said to his mother, who was peering into the blender, "They want to get here at twelve for an early lunch."

His mother did not reply.

"What are you going to give them for starters?" said Mr. Crask from the doorway.

"Andrew! Daphne is your *sister!* The Bewdleys do *not* rate *hors d'oeuvres.*"

"Well, I'd have thought you could give them *something.* Stuffed tomatoes or *something,* " said Mr. Crask as he went up the front path, kicking the heap of shells out of his way.

George washed his hands, stuck a Band-Aid on the worst of the cuts, and slotted the cat flap into its frame.

Mrs. Crask cut up the windfall apples and put them into a pie dish.

The sky clouded over and a light rain started to fall.

"They won't want to go to the beach in this," said Mrs. Crask, looking out.

"Oh, heavens! We'll have them for the whole afternoon!" groaned George.

There was a sudden outburst of screeching and caterwauling from the garden. The fat black tom shot through George's new cat flap, pursued by the tough tabby from three houses away.

The house seemed full of cats. They went skittering upstairs.

"Where's Mishkin?" said Mrs. Crask.

Mishkin was outside the cat flap, wailing pitifully. He did not know how to use it.

"Look, you dumb oaf, you do it like this," George told him. "Put your nose under the flap and *tip* it *up.*"

He demonstrated over and over, he held Mishkin up to the flap, he pushed him through, he pulled him through. Mishkin still totally failed to grasp the principle.

"Try cutting a slit in a cork and sticking it on the side of the flap to hold it open," suggested Mrs. Crask. "I've heard that helps. Oh, *heavens*, my stew!"

She snatched it off the stove.

"Has it dried up?"

"A bit. Not too bad."

"Put some orange soda in it," suggested George, slicing a cork with a razor blade. The fat black tom bolted past him, making its getaway, and he cut his thumb.

Mishkin sat inside the cat flap and wailed.

"I'm fed up!" said George suddenly. "I'm going to turn into a tree."

He went out onto the damp front lawn. From his trouser pocket he took a small tube of water. He poured some of the water onto his shoes.

"George!" shouted his mother through the window. "Don't be silly!"

George took no notice.

He stood motionless on the grass, with his arms out sideways, hands curved upwards to catch the rain.

The telephone rang.

Mrs. Crask put her stew back on the stove and went to answer it.

"Oh—Hello, Daphne. Yes indeed, and how are you? *What?* You think you won't come after all? Oh—to lunch. The girls want to go to a McDonald's? *I* see. But you'd like to come to supper instead? Yes. Yes, of course. No—no—not the least bit in the world."

Slowly Mrs. Crask put the receiver down. A tremendous racket of screeches and caterwauling came from the garden. Mrs. Crask looked out of the kitchen window. A new tree, a well-grown young cherry, was to be seen in the middle of the front lawn. Mishkin had run up it and was crouched in the fork, defying his pursuers.

"George!!!"

George did not answer.

"Where's that little tube?" said Mrs. Crask.

When Mr. Crask came home with his cigarettes, the house was quite silent. Rain fell steadily. The stew bubbled gently on top of the stove. A delicious looking, orange-flavored apple pie stood cooling on the kitchen table.

And two new trees were growing on the front lawn.

"He"

This is my great-aunt Gisela's story. She told me how she learned to be a witch—I suppose you could call it that—from the old lady, Mrs. Polaner. And she passed the information on to me. It was on one of the many occasions when she was trying to teach me embroidery.

I came over from Poland on a ship (said my great-aunt Gisela). It was about seventy years ago—maybe more. I don't remember exactly. I was twelve or thirteen at the time. Warsaw? I can remember a lot of spires—steeples. Gilded. And the smell of the lilacs in the park across the road from our apartment. In the spring I and my friends nearly went mad with the scent—we'd be running across the road all day long to push our noses into the great pink clusters. No cars in those days—only horse-drawn cabs and not many of them. The roads were empty, mostly unpaved, and smelt of horse dung.

Well. My parents died and my grandmother was looking after me. And her two elder sons, my uncles Casimir and Jan, the ones who had gone to America, they wrote and told her to come over and bring me. They had their own businesses, a tobacco shop each, in White Plains, near New York. I quite looked forward to White Plains. Snowy and smooth, I thought it would be, like the country near Byalystok where we went to visit out cousins at Christmas. So we closed up the apartment and sold a lot of things, and we left. I was sad to say good-bye to my friends. My grandmother took various things with her —the two wooden chopping bowls and two pairs of big brass candlesticks and her meat grinder; and we had all our clothes, of course—two big bundles.

The ship was dreadful. We traveled steerage. There were two big cabins, one for men, one for women, with compartments round the walls like stables. Mothers, babies, children, screaming, smells. We didn't go into the men's cabin, of course; the sounds and smells that came out of it were even worse than ours.

Grandmother and I shared a compartment with Mrs. Polaner, another lady, who came from a village deep in the country. She had a firm brown face like an almond shell, and her hair—thick, white, beautiful, it was—pulled back into a big knob at the back. Like grandmother she was wearing lots and lots of clothes, layers and layers, so that she looked even bigger and more massive than she really was, and could only move quite slowly about the ship.

In any case, there was no place we could move *to:* only a tiny patch of deck was left for us steerage passengers. And unless you sat up nearly all night to keep a couple of square feet, the deck was all taken by seven in the morning. People were desperate to get into the fresh air out of the stink and row down below.

Luckily I can say it was a calm passage. What it would have been like if a storm had blown up! But all the way over— weeks, weeks, and weeks, the trip seemed to take—skies were calm and blue from morning to night. And after dark a great moon shone—a harvest moon, a hunter's moon. Mrs. Polaner used to say it made her homesick for her village, which was called Prznov, way out on the great empty plains.

"It's hard to believe that moon is shining over Prznov too," she used to say, sighing.

My grandmother never slept much; she hadn't the least objection to sitting up all night, so she'd stay up, wrapped in shawls and jackets, to keep a place for me and Mrs. Polaner, and we'd come up there after we'd eaten our porridge, and Grandmother would go down for hers. This used to annoy other passengers, but after all, it was our right, wasn't it? The place had been kept for us. Still, there was no real trouble till we reached Galway. Our ship went round by this port on the west coast of Ireland to pick up more passengers—Irish emigrants going to America.

Well. We had thought that we were poor and threadbare enough. But we were like millionaires, we were like Marie Antoinette and all her court, compared with those wild Irish. They came on board barefoot, gazing about them like jungle animals that have been rounded up by the hunter. They were in rags, hardly that, their heads were shaggy, they had no belongings, many of them spoke a language that nobody could understand. They *smelled* wild and strange—of smoke and turf and bog water and dung. Their eyes were blue and rolling—like bits of the sky; they seemed to have no focus.

During the time we spent sailing between Gdansk and Galway, a kind of rough order had grown up in the steerage cabins; passengers knew their own piece of territory and kept to it. And in the morning and at night when we lined up with our bowls for hot water and food, it was understood that places were kept and each person waited in line for his proper turn.

But the Irish soon made havoc of all that; they were used to fighting for all they had; they simply could not comprehend that there might be other ways of doing things. The women pushed in front with elbows and fists, battling to be first for whatever was coming, and the men were drunk most of the time, from mysterious bottles and brews they had brought with them—they were yelling and singing, dancing and fighting, from dawn to dusk. Also, they were all dirty, they brought on board with them lice, fleas, and filth: in half a day we were all itching and scratching, and with so little space, so little soap, so little washing water, there was nothing to be done about it. That was the worst of all. It was dreadful to feel dirty, scurfy, verminous, to see bugs crawling up the wall, and still, outside, the calm blue sea going past, so clean and huge, the great white moon overhead, so shining and pure.

Well. Before the Irish came on board, Mrs. Polaner had been used to talking to me all day long in our patch of the sun on the deck. What did she talk about? I hardly remember. She was a country person—she knew about country things. She had her own wisdom. Her words were like weather—they seemed to come from outside her, like wind, like waves. She would never say, "I like fish," "I had a blue dress," "My husband was unkind to me"; the things she had to tell came from a distance, they were blown to her, or time brought them.

After the Irish came we had no peace on deck any more. Our small patch was disputed all day long. And also Mrs. Polaner felt sick. The way it happened was like this. Among the Irish passengers there were a number of boys, and many of these had brought things they called their hurley sticks. They were curved sticks, intended to play a game with a ball, but of course there was no place on board to play their game, and the sticks were nothing but a nuisance; the boys would have them up on deck and use them to hit each other, and the sticks would get dropped and lie about among the coils of rope, a danger to everybody, for they would roll and slide under your foot and trip you up. The boys fought endless battles, hitting and thrusting at each other's heads and legs like mad beasts.

There was a big redheaded wild boy, the leader of one of their gangs, and one day, while I was up on deck with Mrs. Polaner, he came charging in our direction, after another boy, and, aiming a swipe at his enemy, he caught Mrs. Polaner a terrible blow on her leg that turned her white with pain. Not so much as a word of apology did the heathen give her but went stampeding on his way shouting out, "Yerragh, come back here till I paste the liver and lights out of ye!" Nor did he favor us with so much as a backward look to see what harm he had done.

Mrs. Polaner was never the same after that day. The bruise did not heal as it should; her leg swelled up, turned a frightening purple color, and was so tender that even a piece of lint laid across it made her bite her lips and cry out. She could not manage to walk up on deck any longer—it hurt her too dreadfully to move—so my grandmother and I took turns staying with her down below. And she began refusing to eat—all she would touch was milk.

"No, child, I mustn't eat," she'd say, so decisively that it was difficult arguing with her. Impossible, really. It didn't seem *she* had made up her mind—it had been made up for her, as if a shoot had come out of the ground or a branch broken off a tree.

Soon she was delirious with the pain and would lie in her bunk, moving restlessly, to and fro, to and fro, like an animal, rambling on all the time about owls and the moon and nightingales, begging me not to forget to feed the geese, pick the blackcurrants, fetch in the bracken for the fowls, carry water for the washing, pile thorn bushes in the gap to stop the pigs from getting out, remember to cross yourself when you see the new moon, hang the first tassel of corn on the big oak in the forest, fetch Uncle Anatol to shoot the hare that was sitting in the middle of the beet field, spread out the men's shirts on the grass to bleach, carry a cheese and a pail of water to the haymakers in the far meadow, curtsy and kiss your hand to the rainbow, drop a handful of salt into the spring as a gift for the water fairy and ask her not to let it freeze in winter or dry up in summer, watch for the swallows who will soon be coming back and put out a baking of bread to make them bring good weather on their wings. . . . On and on it went. Sitting by her, giving her little sips of water, I could almost forget where I was—I hardly noticed the throb of the ship, mothers shouting, children wailing, the heat, and the disgusting smell—I was in a world of great corn fields and little thatched houses, huge quiet oak forests and wide rivers.

My grandmother wanted to fetch the ship's doctor, but Mrs. Polaner would not allow that.

"First let me look in my black box," she said. (This was during a clear spell when she was out of her delirium.)

"Box, what box?" said my grandmother.

"Bring my bundle here," ordered Mrs. Polaner. She was too weak to undo it herself, but my grandmother and I unwound the hard mass of shawls and petticoats and, right in the middle, from a tight coil of old yellow linen, we found a little worn black wooden box, like a snuffbox, not as big as my clenched fist.

Mrs. Polaner said, "My great-grandfather once served a nobleman, Count Mieszo-Zbigniew. He saved the Count's life, one time, from a wild boar in a forest. As a reward the Count gave him this box, which one of his ancestors had brought back from the Holy Land. It was made from a tree that grew by the Holy Sea; long ago, hundreds and hundreds of years, there was sand from that sea inside it. The sand has long ago trickled away . . . but still you can feel the dust of it on your finger, and if you look into the box for a while, you can see the sand begin to move."

"I see no sand," said my grandmother, opening the box. But Mrs. Polaner took it and looked into it.

"I am not to have the doctor," she said after a while in a low voice. "He could not help me; I am to die."

This made my grandmother very angry. Mrs. Polaner was her friend, her only friend on the ship; she did not intend to lose her so easily. She said it was wrong to die when one might be saved.

"I cannot be saved," Mrs. Polaner said. "It would waste the doctor's time to come."

However my grandmother paid no heed to this, and the doctor was sent for. He had so many sick people to see that he did not come for another two days; meanwhile Mrs. Polaner's face became very pinched, her mouth sank back between deep grooves, and her brown skin turned a bluish white.

When he did come at last, the doctor looked at her rather

hopelessly and said she should have milk and fresh air; he ordered a hammock to be slung for her on deck.

This was done, and my grandmother and I sat by her and took turns going to the galley to fetch her milk. Milk she would take and seemed to enjoy: "Ah," she said once thoughtfully as she sipped it, "this is from Jadwiga, I can always tell; she is the best cow in the herd."

Well, one time when I was bringing her a cup of milk that same big redheaded lout came charging past me, chasing one of his friends as usual, and knocked my arm so that I spilled half the cupful.

"Mind where you go, you heathen monster!" I shouted after him, and at that he turned around and looked at me scornfully up and down, and then he came back and grabbed me by the pigtail. My hair was yellow in those days, and I had a wooden buckle that my uncle Boleslaw had carved for me to keep it in place. This the Irish boy pulled off and threw it over the side, into the water; and then with a loud stupid laugh he ran off after his friend.

I was so upset and furious that my hands were shaking as I took the milk to Mrs. Polaner, and I spilled some more of it.

She was tossing and muttering about a forest of yew trees, a great forest where the bison still wander, but she came back from that distance when I put my hands round the warm cup, and said, "What is the matter, little one? Why are your cheeks so red, Gisela, and your eyes so angry?"

"That boy—that boy who hit you," I mumbled. "I'd like—I'd like to make him sorry—I'd like to see *him* lying on the deck with a hurt leg."

"Oh, it could be done, it could be done, you could do it," said Mrs. Polaner, "but what is the good? The box can do such things, but power should be used in a different way. Trees do not fight each other. One river does not flow into another's bed. The hills do not go marching into the plain. Leave him alone; he is only a stupid boy."

But I wanted to know what she meant.

"The *box* would do it, Mrs. Polaner? Please explain. How could the box do it?"

"Write on a slip of paper—"

"Write? Write what?"

"The name—the person's name—put in the box—" Mrs. Polaner was drowsy, slipping off again; soon she cried out, "The spruce trees, look, they are all covered with ivy, we must pull the ivy down from the spruce trees," and she began trying to climb out of her hammock. Her head was so hot that it felt like a live coal, and we had to hold her down.

That night she died. Before she went she was clear and calm; she saw my grandmother and said, "I am sorry to leave you, Magda my friend, but I do not think I should have enjoyed living in a town. I am going back to the forests; they are what suit me best. You can keep my bundle for yourself; only see my son's wife has the amber necklace, but she won't want my petticoats, I am sure of that." To me she said, "The black box is for you, little one, but use it sensibly; a fire once lit is not easy to put out."

Then she closed her eyes and left us.

When the ship's nurse came to help my grandmother carry Mrs. Polaner down and perform the last offices, I slipped away with the little black box and went on deck again. I did not know the redheaded boy's name, so I got a piece of paper and simply wrote on it, *"He."* I thought the box would know its business. There would be no need to tell it. And indeed it did. The very next day my redhead tripped over another boy's hurley stick and fell sprawling. When he tried to get up he groaned and fell back again; watching from a distance, I saw when the doctor was fetched and told him that his leg was broken. How I laughed—or rather, tried to laugh; I was feeling too sad, really, because of Mrs. Polaner, and could only find a bitter, angry pleasure at his punishment. The doctor put his leg in a great white plaster cast, all the way down to the ankle, and it was some satisfaction to see his impatience and rage as he hopped clumsily about, using his hurley stick as a crutch.

I would have liked to go up to him and say, "*I* did that to you, *I* did it!" but I did not quite have the courage. He was so big and active, even now, in spite of his broken leg; he still looked dangerous. Besides, he would not have believed me.

After a day or two, though, a change came over him. He began to complain that the plaster cast itched abominably on his leg. "That is because it catches on the hairs of your skin," the doctor said. "Don't make such a fuss about it—everybody has to bear that with a cast. You'll just have to put up with it."

Nevertheless the boy—I never did learn his name—cursed and screamed; he said the torture of the plaster was worse than fire burning, worse than having his skin stripped off, he could not stand the pain, it was not to be endured.

"Aha," I thought, "now the box is really beginning to work; now you begin to understand what you did to Mrs. Polaner in your stupid carelessness." And I gloated as he hobbled about, frantically rubbing the outside of the plaster, as if that would relieve the itching inside.

After another day or two he was not to be seen on deck but lay in the men's cabin, and sometimes we could hear him shrieking; a terrible sound it was, hardly human, more like an animal being killed. Then I felt sorry for what I had done and took the paper out of the box and threw it in the sea.

I had left it too late, though, for the boy died. We heard that the doctor, puzzled by his death, ordered the plaster cast taken off. They found that his leg had been eaten away inside the plaster by bugs, almost to the bone; that was what had caused the pain.

Two days later we reached Ellis Island, where the immigrants all landed; and when we had gone through the immigration building, there were my uncles Casimir and Jan, waiting to meet us.

I still had the box. I had been so frightened of its power that I thought of throwing it into the sea, after the boy died; I could see what Mrs. Polaner had meant when she said "Power should be used in a different way." But then I thought that if I threw it into the sea it might be angry with me; it might do me some harm; so in the end I kept it.

But I never used it again.

That was my great-aunt Gisela's story that she told me as she embroidered a pillowcase. She never married but became housekeeper to a Polish priest, and lived in Boston all her life.

When she was lying on her deathbed, she kept calling out:

"Ask him to forgive me! Ask him, please ask him! He is standing there, he is there! What *he* did was an accident, but what *I* did was on purpose. Tell him I am sorry!"

"Tell who, Aunt Gisela?" said my mother, who was with her. "Who is standing there?"

"He is!" cried Aunt Gisela. "*He!*"

Then she died.

I have the box now, but, unlike Aunt Gisela, I have never dared to use it.

Time to Laugh

When Matt climbed in at the open window of The Croft, it had been raining steadily for three days—August rain, flattening the bronze-green plains of wheat, making dim green jungles of the little woods around Wentby, turning the highway which cut across the small town's southern tip into a greasy nightmare on which traffic skidded and piled into crunching heaps; all the county police were desperately busy trying to clear up one disaster after another.

If there had been a river at Wentby, Matt might have gone fishing instead, on that Saturday afternoon . . . but the town's full name was Wentby Waterless, the nearest brook was twenty miles away, the rain lay about in scummy pools on the clay or sank into the lighter soil and vanished. And if the police had not been so manifestly engaged and distracted by the highway chaos, it might never have occurred to Matt that now would be the perfect time to explore The Croft; after all, by the end of three days' rain, what else was there to do? It had been ten years since the Regent Cinema closed its doors for the last time and went into liquidation.

A high school duffel coat would be too conspicuous and recognizable; Matt wore his black plastic jacket, although it was not particularly rainproof. But it was at least some protection against the brambles which barred his way.

He had long ago worked out an entry into the Croft grounds, having noticed that they ended in a little triangle of land which bit into the corner of a builder's yard where his father had once briefly worked; Matt had a keen visual memory, never forgot anything he had once observed, and, after a single visit two years ago to tell his father that Mom had been taken off to the hospital, was able to pick his way without hesitation through cement mixers, stacks of two-by-twos, and concrete slabs to the exact corner, the wattle pickets and tangle of elderberry bushes. Kelly never troubled to lock his yard, and, in any case, on a Saturday afternoon no one was about; they were all snug at home, watching TV.

He bored his way through the wet greenery and, as he had reckoned, came to the weed-smothered terrace at the foot of a flight of steps; overgrown shoots of rambler rose half blocked them, but it was just possible to battle upwards, and at the top he was rewarded by a dusky, triangular vista of lawn stretching away on the left toward the house, on the right toward untended vegetable gardens. Amazingly—in the very middle of Wentby—there were rabbits feeding on the lawn, who scattered at his appearance. And between him and the house, two aged, enormous apple trees towered, massive against the murky sky, loaded down with fruit. He had seen them in the aerial photographs of the town recently exhibited on a school notice board: that was what had given him the notion of exploring The Croft; you could find out a few things at school if you kept your eyes open and used your wits. He had heard of The Croft before that, of course, but it was nowhere to be seen from any of the town streets: a big house, built in the mid-nineteenth century on an inaccessible plot of land, bought subsequently, after World War Two, by a rich old retired actress and her company-director husband, Lieutenant-Colonel and Mrs. Jordan. They were hardly ever seen; never came out or went anywhere; Matt had a vague idea that one of them—maybe both?—had died. There was a general belief that the house was haunted; also full of treasures; also defended by any number of burglar alarms inside the building, gongs that would start clanging, bells that would ring up at the police station, not to mention man-traps, spring guns, and savage german shepherds outside in the grounds.

However the german shepherds did not seem to be in evidence—if they had been, surely the rabbits would not have been feeding so peacefully? So, beginning to disbelieve these tales, Matt picked his way, quietly but with some confidence, over the sodden tussocky grass to the apple trees. The fruit, to his chagrin, was far from ripe. Also they were wretched little apples, sour cooking apples possibly, lumpy and misshapen, not worth the bother of stealing. Even the birds appeared to have neglected them; numbers of undersized windfalls lay rotting already on the ground. Angrily, Matt flung a couple against the wall of the house, taking some satisfaction from the squashy thump with which they spattered the stone. The house had not been built of local brick like the rest of Wentby, but from massive chunks of somber, liver-colored rock, imported, no doubt at great expense, from farther north. The effect was powerful and ugly; dark as blood, many-gabled and frowning, the building kept guard over its tangled grounds. It seemed deserted; all the windows were lightless, even on such a pouring wet afternoon; and, prowling around to the front of the house, over a carriage-drive pocked with grass and weeds, Matt found that the front doorstep had a thin skin of moss over it, as if no foot had trodden there for months. Perhaps the back—? But that was some distance away and behind a screen of trelliswork and yellow-flecked ornamental laurels. Working on toward it, Matt came to a stop, badly startled at the sight of a half-open window, which, until he reached it, had been concealed from him by a great sagging swatch of untrimmed winter jasmine, whose tiny dark green leaves were almost black with wet. The coffin-shaped oblong of the open window was black too; Matt stared at it, hypnotized, for almost five minutes, unable to decide whether to go in or not.

Was there somebody inside, there, in the dark? Or had the house been burgled, maybe weeks ago, and the burglar had left the window like that, not troubling to conceal the evidence of his entry, because nobody ever came to the place? Or—unnerving thought—was there a burglar inside now, at this minute?

Revolving all these different possibilities, Matt found that he had been moving slowly nearer and nearer to the wall with the window in it; the window was about six feet above ground but so thickly sleeved around with creeper that climbing in would present no problem at all. The creeper seemed untouched, showed no sign of damage.

Almost without realizing that he had come to a decision, Matt found himself digging his toes into the wet mass and pulling himself up—showers of drops flew into his face—until he was able to lean across the windowsill, bracing his elbows against the inner edge of the frame. As might have been expected, the sill inside was swimming with rainwater, the paint starting to crack; evidently the window had been open for hours, maybe days.

Matt stared into the dusky interior, waiting for his eyes to adjust to the dimness. At first, all he could see was vague masses of furniture. Slowly these began to resolve into recognizable forms: tapestried chairs with high backs and bulbous curving legs, side tables covered in ornaments, a standard lamp with an elaborate pleated shade, dripping tassels, a huge china pot, a flower-patterned carpet, a black shaggy hearthrug, a gold-framed portrait over the mantel. The hearth was fireless, the chair beside it empty, the room sunk in silence. Listening with all his concentration, Matt could hear no sound from anywhere about the house. Encouraged, he swung a knee over the sill, ducked his head and shoulders under the sash, and levered himself in; then, with instinctive caution, he slid down the sash behind him, so that, in the unlikely event of another intruder visiting the garden, the way indoors would not be so enticingly visible.

Matt did not intend to close the window completely, but the sash cord had perished, and the heavy frame, once in motion, shot right down before he could stop it; somewhat to his con-

sternation, a little catch clicked across; evidently it was a bur-
glar-proof lock, for he was unable to pull it open again; there
was a keyhole in the catch, and he guessed that it could not
now be opened again without the key.

Swearing under his breath, Matt turned to survey the room.
How would it ever be possible to find the right key in this
cluttered, dusty place? It might be in a bowl of odds and ends
on the mantelpiece—or in a desk drawer—or hanging on a nail
—or in a box—no casual intruder could hope to come across it.
Nor—he turned back to inspect the window again—could he
hope to smash his way out. The windowpanes were too small,
the bars too thick. Still, there would be other ways of leaving
the house; perhaps he could simply unlock an outside door. He
decided that before exploring any farther he had better estab-
lish his means of exit and so took a couple of steps toward a
doorway that he could now see on his right. This led through
to a large chilly dining room where a cobwebbed chandelier
hung over a massive mahogany dining table, corralled by eight
chairs, and reflecting ghostly gray light from a window beyond. The dining room window, to Matt's relief, was a casement; easy enough to break out of that, he thought, his spirits
rising. But perhaps there would be no need; perhaps the burglar catch was not fastened, and he was about to cross the
dining room and examine it closely when the sound of silvery
laughter behind him nearly shocked him out of his wits.

"Aha! Aha! Ha-ha-ha-ha-ha-ha!" trilled the mocking voice,
not six feet away. Matt spun around, his heart almost bursting
out through his rib cage. He would have been ready to swear
there wasn't a soul in the house. Was it a ghost? Were the
stories true, after all?

The room he had first entered still seemed empty, but the
laughter had certainly come from that direction, and as he
stood in the doorway, staring frantically about him, he heard
it again, a long mocking trill, repeated in exactly the same
cadence.

"Jesus!" whispered Matt.

And then, as he honestly thought he was on the point of fainting from fright, the explanation was supplied. At exactly the same point from which the laughter had come, a clock began to chime in a thin silvery note obviously intended to match the laughter: *ting, tong, ting, tong.* Four o'clock.

"Jesus," breathed Matt again. "How about that? A laughing clock!"

He moved over to inspect the clock. It was a large, elaborate affair, stood on a kind of bureau with brass handles, under a glass dome. The structure of the clock, outworks, whatever you call it, was all gilded and ornamented with gold cherubs who were falling about laughing, throwing their fat little heads back or doubled up with amusement.

"Very funny," muttered Matt sourly. "Almost had me dead of heart failure, you can laugh!"

Over the clock, he now saw, a big tapestry hung on the wall, which echoed the theme of laughter: girls in frilly tunics this time and a fat old man sitting on a barrel squashing grapes into his mouth while he hugged a girl to him with the other arm; all of them, too, splitting themselves over some joke, probably a rude one to judge from the old fellow's appearance.

Matt wished very much that the clock would strike again, but presumably it would not do that till five o'clock—unless it chimed the quarters; he had better case the rest of the house in the meantime and reckon to be back in this room by five. Would it be possible to pinch the clock? he wondered. But it looked dauntingly heavy—and probably its mechanism was complicated and delicate, might go wrong if shifted; how could he ever hope to carry it through all those bushes and over the picket fence? And then there would be the problem of explaining its appearance in his father's small apartment; he could hardly say that he had found it lying on a rubbish dump. Still he longed to possess it—think what the other guys in the gang would say when they heard it! Maybe he could keep it in Kip Butterworth's house—old Kip, lucky fellow, had a room of his own and such a lot of electronic junk all over it that one clock more or less would never be noticed.

But first he would bring Kip here, at a time just before the clock was due to strike, and let *him* have the fright of his life. . . .

Sniggering to himself at this agreeable thought, Matt turned back toward the dining room, intending to carry out his original plan of unfastening one of the casement windows, when for the second time he was stopped dead by terror.

A voice behind him said, "Since you are here, you may as well wind the clock." And added dryly, "Saturday is its day for winding, so it is just as well you came."

This time the voice was unmistakably human; trembling like a leaf, Matt was obliged to admit to himself that there was no chance of its being some kind of electronic device—or even a ghost. It was an old woman's voice, harsh, dry, a little shaky, but resonant; only, where the devil *was* she?

Then he saw that what he had taken for a wall beyond the fireplace was, in fact, one of those dangling bamboo curtains, and beyond it—another bad moment for Matt—was this motionless figure sitting on a chair, watching him, had been watching him—must have—all the time, ever since he had climbed in, for the part of the room beyond the curtain was just a kind of alcove, a big bay window really, leading nowhere. She must have been there all the time. . . .

"Go on," she repeated, watching Matt steadily from out of her black triangles of eyes, "wind the clock."

He found his voice and said hoarsely, "Where's the key, then?"

"In the round bowl on the left side."

His heart leaped; perhaps the window key would be there too. But it was not; there was only one key: a long, heavy brass shaft with a cross piece at one end and a lot of fluting at the other.

"Lift the dome off carefully," she said. "You'll find two keyholes in the face. Wind them both. One's for the clock, the other for the chime."

And, as he lifted off the dome and began winding, she added thoughtfully, "My husband made that clock for me, on my thirtieth birthday. It's a recording of my own voice—the laugh. Uncommon, isn't it? He was an electrical engineer, you see. Clocks were his hobby. All kinds of unusual ones he invented—there was a Shakespearean clock and a barking dog and one that sang hymns—my voice again. I had a beautiful singing voice in those days—and my laugh was famous of course. 'Miss Langdale's crystalline laugh,' the critics used to call it. . . . My husband was making a skull clock just before he died. There's the skull."

There it was, to be sure, and a real skull, perched on top of the big china jar to the right of the clock.

Vaguely now, Matt remembered reports of her husband's death; wasn't there something a bit odd about it? Found dead of heart failure in the underpass below the highway, at least a mile from his house; what had he been *doing* there, in the middle of the night? Why walk through the underpass, which was not intended for pedestrians anyway?

"He was going to get some cigarettes when he died," she went on, and Matt jumped; had she read his thoughts? How could she know so uncannily what was going through his head?

"I've given up smoking since then," she went on. "Had to, really. . . . They won't deliver, you see. Some things you can get delivered, so I make do with what I can get. I don't like people coming to the house too often because they scare the birds. I'm a great bird person, you know—"

Unless she has a servant, then, she's alone in the house, Matt thought, as she talked on, in her sharp, dry old voice. He began to feel less terrified—perhaps he could just scare her into letting him leave. Perhaps, anyway, she was mad?

"Are you going to phone the police?" he asked boldly. "I

wasn't going to pinch anything, you know—just came in to
have a look-see."

"My dear boy, I don't care *why* you came in. As you *are* here,
you might as well make yourself useful. Go into the dining
room, will you, and bring back some of those bottles."

The rain had abated, just a little, and the dining room was
some degrees lighter when he walked through into it. All
along the window wall Matt was amazed to see wooden wine-
racks filled with bottles and half-bottles of champagne. There
must be hundreds. There were also, in two large log baskets
beside the empty grate, dozens of empties. An armchair was
drawn close to an electric heater, not switched on; a half-
empty glass and bottle stood on a silver tray on the floor beside
the armchair.

"Bring a glass, too," Mrs. Jordan called.

And, when he returned with the glass, the tray, and several
bottles under his arm, she said. "Now, open one of them. You
know how to, I hope?"

He had seen it done on TV; he managed it without difficulty.

"Ought to be chilled, of course," she remarked, receiving
the glass from him. One of her hands lay limply on the arm of
the chair—she hitched it up from time to time with the other
hand when it slipped off; and, now that he came near to her
for the first time, he noticed that she smelled very bad; a
strange, fetid smell of dry, unwashed old age and something
worse. He began to suspect that perhaps she was *unable* to
move from her chair. Curiously enough, instead of this making him fear her less, it made him fear her more. Although she
seemed a skinny, frail old creature, her face was quite full in
shape, pale and puffy like underdone pastry. It must have been
handsome once—long ago—like a wicked fairy pretending to
be a princess in a kid's book illustration; now she just looked
spiteful and secretive, grinning down at her glass of bubbly.
Her hair, the color of old dry straw, was done very fancy,
piled up on top of her head. Perhaps it was a wig?

"Get a glass for yourself, if you want," she said. "There are some more in the dining room cupboard."

He half thought of zipping out through the dining-room window while he was in there; but still, he was curious to try the fizz and there didn't seem to be any hurry, really. It was pretty plain the old girl wasn't going anywhere, couldn't be any actual danger to him, although she did rather give him the gooeys. Also he did want to hear that chime again.

As he was taking a glass out from the shimmering ranks in the cupboard, a marvelous thought struck him: Why not bring all the gang here for a banquet? Look at those hundreds and hundreds of bottles of champagne—what a waste, not to make use of them! Plainly *she* was never going to get through them all—not in the state she was in. Maybe he could find some canned stuff in the house too—but anyway, they could bring their own grub with them, hamburgers and fries or stuff from the Chinese takeout—if the old girl was actually paralyzed in her chair, she couldn't stop them. . . . In fact it would add to the fun, the excitement, having her there. They could fetch her in from the next room, drink her health in her own bubbly; better not leave it too long, though, didn't seem likely she could last more than a few more days.

Candles, he thought, we'd have to bring candles; and at that point her voice cut into his thoughts, calling, "Bring the two candles that are standing on the cupboard."

He started violently—but it was only a coincidence, after all —picked up the candles in their tall cut-glass sticks and carried them next door with a glass for himself.

"Matches on the mantel," she said.

The matches were in a fancy enamel box. He lit the candles and put them on the little table beside her. Now he could see more plainly that there was something extremely queer about her: her face was all drawn down one side, and half of it didn't seem to work very well.

"Electricity cut off," she said. "Forgot to pay the bill."

Her left hand was still working all right, and she had swallowed down two glasses in quick succession, refilling them herself each time from the opened bottle at her elbow. "Fill your glass," she said, slurring the words a little.

He was very thirsty—smoked fish and baked beans they always had for Saturday midday dinner, and the fright had dried up his mouth too—like Mrs. Jordan he tossed down two glasses one after the other. They fizzed a bit—otherwise they didn't have much taste.

"Better open another bottle," she said. "One doesn't go anywhere between two. Fetch in a few more while you're up, why don't you."

She's planning, he thought to himself; knows she can't move from that chair, so she wants to be stocked up for when I've gone. He wondered if in fact there was a phone in the house? Ought he to ring for a doctor, the police, an ambulance? But then he would have to account for his presence. And he and the gang would never get to have their banquet; the windows would be boarded up for sure; she'd be carted off to the Royal West Midland geriatric ward, like Auntie Glad after her stroke.

"There isn't a phone in the house," said Mrs. Jordan calmly. "I had it taken out after Jock died; the bell disturbed the birds. —That's right, put them all down by my chair, where I can reach them."

He opened another bottle, filled both their glasses, then went back to the other room for a third load.

"You like the clock, don't you," she said, as he paused by it, coming back.

"Yeah. It's uncommon."

"It'll strike the quarter in a minute," she said, and soon it did—a low, rather malicious chuckle, just a brief spurt of sound. It made the hair prickle on the back of Matt's neck, but he thought again, Just wait till the rest of the gang hears that! A really spooky sound.

"I don't want you making off with it, though," she said.

"No, no, that would never do. I like to sit here and listen to it."

"I wasn't going to take it!"

"No, well, that's as may be." Her triangular black eyes in their hollows laughed down at him—he was squatting on the carpet near her chair, easing out a particularly obstinate cork. "I'm not taking any chances. Eight days—that clock goes for eight days. Did you wind up the chime too?"

"Yeah, yeah," he said impatiently, tipping more straw-colored fizz into their glasses. Through the pale liquid in the glass he still seemed to see her eyes staring at him shrewdly.

"Put your glass down a moment," she said. "On the floor—that will do. Now, just look here a moment." She was holding up her skinny forefinger. Past it he could see those two dark triangles. "That's right. Now—watch my finger—you are very tired, aren't you? You are going to lie down on the floor and go to sleep. You will sleep—very comfortably—for ten minutes. When you wake, you will walk over to that door and lock it. The key is in the lock. Then you will take out the key and push it under the door with one of the knitting needles that are lying on the small table by the door. Ahhh! You are so sleepy." She yawned, deeply. Matt was yawning too. His head flopped sideways on to the carpet, and he lay motionless, deep asleep.

While he slept it was very quiet in the room. The house was too secluded in its own grounds among the builder's yards for any sound from the town to reach it; only faintly from far away came the throb of the highway. Mrs. Jordan sat impassively listening to it. She did not sleep; she had done enough sleeping and soon would sleep even deeper. She sat listening and thinking about her husband; sometimes the lopsided smile crooked down one corner of her mouth.

After ten minutes the sleeping boy woke up. Drowsily he staggered to his feet, walked over to the door, locked it, removed the key, and, with a long wooden knitting needle, thrust it far underneath and out across the polished dining room floor.

Returning to the old lady, he stared at her in a vaguely bewildered manner, rubbing one hand up over his forehead.

"My head aches," he said in a grumbling tone.

"You need a drink. Open another bottle," she said. "Listen: the clock is going to strike the half hour."

On the other side of the room the clock gave its silvery chuckle.

Lodgers

"Are you *sure*, doctor?" said Rose Burdock. "You really mean that *he's* got mumps and *she's* got measles? You couldn't be mistaken?"

"No mistake," said Doctor Cobb briskly. "Seen too many cases this week—half the town's got one or the other. Bob's got the stiff neck—Titch has the spots. Nothing you can do but keep 'em warm, give 'em aspirin and lots to drink. Wrap up their necks and ears and keep 'em isolated, because what's sure to happen is that in a couple of weeks they'll swap bugs; it's then you'll *really* have to worry, because they'll be a bit pulled down by the first bug, so they may take the next one harder."

"How long will it last?" she said faintly.

He was scribbling prescriptions. "Umn? Oh, you'll probably have 'em both at home for about a month from first to last. Here, this is for Titch, every four hours round the clock, and these are for Bob, same, till their temperatures are back to normal. Call me if the fever goes on for more than two days or if there is any delirium."

"Delirium!"

"Not likely unless mumps-meningitis sets in. Watch out for bronchitis or pneumonia, though, of course. Have *you* had mumps and measles, by the way?"

"Oh yes."

"Well, you can get mumps again, so look out," he said with callous cheer, running down the front steps. Rose dully watched him go. There was a small disused graveyard beside her house. A heavy rain followed by a sharp January frost had left all the gravestones neatly cased in ice. They looked like playing cards laid out for patience. Patience . . . How peaceful, she thought, to be lying stretched out in one's bones under there, with an ice pack overhead, and went back into the house where Titch, hot and miserable, wanted a drink and to be rubbed with eau de cologne; Bob, feverish, and with acutely painful glands, wanted a hot poultice around his neck to take away the pain; both asked to be read aloud to, and both wished to be made instantly better.

Rose presently dragged herself wearily downstairs for the next disagreeable duty.

"*Woman's Scene*— can I speak to Mrs. Joubert, please?—Mrs. Joubert—this is Rose Burdock, Mrs. Joubert—I am most *terribly* sorry, but it looks as if I shan't be able to get to the office on Monday. Both my children are sick: one with mumps, one with measles, and my lodger left two days ago—I've got no one at home to look after them. —Yes, of *course* I'll try to find somebody over the weekend—of *course* I will. But—yes, I know. Yes, I do realize that. Yes, I *know* Wednesday is press day. I'll certainly see what I can do. I just thought I had better warn you in case—Yes, yes, I will. Yes, of course."

"You do remember, Mrs. Burdock," came the editor's clear voice over the wire, "that when we gave you this job it was on the strict understanding that there were to be no extra days off, no emergencies or crises, that if you came to us you promised *never* to leave us in the lurch on press days?"

Rose remembered the conversation extremely well. Mrs. Joubert, who had a face like an isosceles triangle on its apex with a crest of blue hair and two zero signs for eyes, had terrified her so much that she had made the promise unhesitatingly with every intention of keeping it. Besides, with a well-disposed lodger who was always home in the afternoon before the children had finished school, the future had seemed secure. Who could have foretold that the lodger would be summoned to Scotland to nurse a dying mother or that the children would succumb to mumps and measles simultaneously?

"I'll do my very best, Mrs. Joubert," she said in despair.

"Please do, dear. Because this sort of thing really mustn't happen, you know. We've been *very* good to you—made special arrangements for you to work a four-day week—"

"Yes—I know—"

"Very well then."

After the formidable click with which Mrs. Joubert rang off came the immediate peal of the front doorbell. Oh god, now what? Rose thought, and dragged herself to the door. If that's the meter man, it means another electricity bill.

It was not the meter man, but a frail-looking woman with badly waved hair dangling on either side of her face like a cocker spaniel's ears. Her face was somehow ineffectual—pale and long, with anxious gray eyes and a mouth that made efforts to be firm but kept dropping back into a weakly placating curve. Her skin was dry and chalky, and her clothes hung on her like dead leaves after the first rains of winter.

"Mrs. Burdock?" Her voice was placating too, refined yet shallow, as if she never took in quite enough breath. "You won't know me but I've heard of you through your professional associates—well, through Mrs. Joubert actually—"

"If it's life insurance I'm afraid I'm not interested," said Rose swiftly. "And—you must excuse me, but I've two sick children in the house—I have to get back to them—"

"No, *no*, you misunder*stand* me—I'm giving Mrs. Joubert as a *ref*erence—actually she's a friend of my husband's father, Admiral Colegate at South Dean."

"Oh, I see." In fact Rose saw nothing; it was true that Mrs. Joubert had a weekend cottage at the village of South Dean five miles away, and no doubt she knew dozens of admirals there, but why should that bring this dithering woman to stand on her threshold?

"The fact is, we're a bit desperate, my husband and I," Mrs. Colegate went on rapidly with what she seemed to hope was a winning smile, "and we happened to hear—through the local grapevine you know—that you might have some rooms to let in your house—we wondered if there might be a chance for us to rent them?"

"You want to rent *rooms?*" Suddenly the sunlight on the graveyard's frosted grass seemed to have acquired the heat of midsummer; Mrs. Colegate's chalky face was haloed in a golden fuzz of hair. "Oh, now I do see! Please come in and look at them, won't you? I'm afraid they're nothing very grand —just two rooms, a bathroom, and kitchenette—won't you come upstairs?"

"We don't *want* anything grand," pattered Mrs. Colegate in her soft, conciliating voice, following up the stairs. She had to duck her skimpy length to get in at the spare bedroom door, for the house was Tudor, with lintels to match, and she quite tall; nonetheless she instantly exclaimed, "*Oh,* how delightful! Why, this would suit us down to the *ground!* It's really an answer to prayer, you see, as my husband has been disqualified from driving for six months—just on a technicality, you know, so silly—and he has to catch the eight-fifteen twice a week to town, and there's no bus to South Dean, and I'm a wretched driver in a fog, and you *know* how many fogs we've been having, these mornings—We have been living at South Dean with the Admiral, you see, my husband's father, ever since we had to come back from Iran so suddenly—Desmond had an *excellent* job in Tehran; it was so sad when things got difficult there—"

All this flowed out in a gentle unaccented stream as she, rather inattentively, it seemed to Rose, inspected the bathroom, kitchenette, and two bedsitting rooms. "Quite perfect! And is there a shed or something where we can garage the car?"

That, Rose was obliged to confess, there was not. Her own Mini lived across the lane where there was a slot just big enough for one car—"But I'm afraid they won't allow any more. You can park overnight in the main square, though; that's only three minutes' walk."

Mrs. Colegate declared that that would be absolutely super, and that the whole thing was just what they had been looking for. "Only three minutes to the bus, too—couldn't be more convenient. May we move in this afternoon?"

"Don't you want your husband to come and look first?" said Rose, a little startled.

"No need; no need at all. He'll love it just as much as I do."

"There's just one thing—" Rose hesitated, feeling that, heaven-sent though this chance seemed, it behooved her to be honest. "I have two children aged six and eight—"

"Oh, the *pets!* We *love* children!" cried Mrs. Colegate. "I've had children of my own, you see—grown now, alas!—We shall be so *happy* to live in a house with children once more."

"Oh—that's—I'm very—But the thing is," went on Rose desperately, "that one of my children has mumps at present, and the other has measles, and in about ten days' time or even sooner they are due to reverse the pattern. Are you sure you want to face that? Have you had mumps and measles, Mrs. Colegate?"

"Bless you, yes, my dear, long ago, and so has my husband. Mumps and measles are *nothing* to us! We shall be happy to nurse your children for you. It will make us feel needed; I gather you go up to town every day? I feel quite certain that we are going to fit into your house *very well.* That's all settled, then, and we'll move in this afternoon between three and four —if that is a good time?"

"Yes, of course," Rose said. "I'll give you some keys."

Mrs. Colegate's smile had been so continuous and persevering that it was rather a shock for Rose to observe the violent shaking of her hands as she received the keys. Poor thing, perhaps she had arthritis—or Parkinson's disease, was it, that made the hands shake? Or Somebody's palsy?

"Who was that at the door?" called the children's voices from their separate bedrooms. (It was no use putting them in together: first they argued; then they quarreled; finally they fought.) Rose went to tell them that two new lodgers were due to arrive who would be happy to read aloud, fetch drinks, and do shopping errands. Bob took the news indifferently; he had a temperature of 102°; Titch's face fell.

"I thought *you'd* stay at home to look after us," she said dolefully.

"Honey, you know I'd like to but I can't; I have to go to my office. But I'm sure Mr. and Mrs. Colegate will be very nice. . . ."

At two thirty the bell rang again, and it was a short, very fat man with a green eyeshade over his face, who held an immense, untidy bundle wrapped in a red baize cloth.

"Mrs. Burdock? I'm Desmond Colegate. Delighted to meet you. Can't shake hands, ha, ha. May I carry this little lot upstairs?"

His voice was startlingly high and shrill; the only thing higher, Rose thought, would be a bat's squeak. What she could see of his face, below the green shade, was almost as startlingly white and moist, like the underside of a flounder. Taking her silence for assent, he nipped past her and, locating the stairs by instinct, it seemed, went quickly up with his load. Finding her wits, Rose followed and directed him into the lodgers' rooms.

"Delightful, delightful," he said, dumping the cloth-wrapped bundle on the bed and crossing to the window.

"I'm sorry it looks out on the graveyard," Rose said after clearing her throat. "My son's room does too. I do hope you don't mind."

"*Mind?* Why should I mind? Oh!" he said chuckling, "you mean worry about the spirits of the departed, that sort of thing? But, my dear young lady, that little graveyard is *old*; why, I daresay no one has been buried in it for a hundred years. Nothing spooky is going to come out of there. Dear me, no. A very pleasant prospect. Aha! I believe I hear my wife down below—"

"You mean—only recent graves produce ghosts?" Rose asked, trying for a light note, as she followed him downstairs again.

"Spirits, my dear—spirits! Of course! They wear *out* in the end—burn out, if you like—just like a candle flame. Spirits are not immortal, any more than bodies—they simply have more energy and a longer life span. Thank you, Laura," he added, receiving a plastic garment bag, evidently stuffed with clothes, from his wife, who stood nervously by the open front door. "And of course," he added to Rose, nonplussed in the hall, "it is when they have just left their bodies that spirits are most agitated, not yet knowing, you see, quite where they *stand*, ha, ha!" His chuckle was like ice cubes falling into a glass. He retired up the stairs again with the dress bag and Mrs. Colegate went back to their car, which was parked on the pavement outside with a policeman eyeing it thoughtfully.

"I hope you don't mind our coming a little earlier than we said?" Mrs. Colegate fluttered up the front steps again with a bundle of golf clubs and fishing rods and the hose of a vacuum cleaner. "The Admiral thought it would be more practical to leave during the *daylight;* it gets dark so early these days, and then it's so hard to find things."

She handed the clubs and rods to her husband, who, still in pursuit of his previous theme, said airily, waving a butterfly net, "Yes, yes, spirits, when they have just left their bodies, buzz round in quite a panic—like wasps, you know—positively distilling energy!"

He bustled off up the stairs again—he could move amazingly nimbly for one so fat—calling back what sounded like:

"That's the time to catch them!"

Rose went away into her own kitchen to be by herself. She supposed she had better make the Colegates a cup of tea; that was the proper way to welcome people. She wished that she had not taken such an instantaneous aversion to Desmond Colegate. Probably he was quite ordinary and pleasant when one got to know him; he couldn't help that unnerving voice and fishlike complexion.

During the weekend the Colegates seemed to settle in very completely, in their own way. They had brought no furniture —indeed, they had no need to, for the rooms were furnished— but they had an incredible quantity of paraphernalia, bundles, boxes, rolls, frames, cages, baskets. As they carried these up, Rose could not conceive where they would stow all the stuff in her two moderate-sized rooms, and indeed, when she tapped and entered with the ceremonial cups of tea, the floor was completely covered with objects dumped higgledy-piggledy, and the owners were making no attempt to organize the chaos. They were seated, he on the chaise longue and she on the divan, each with a half-empty glass in hand. A Johnnie Walker bottle stood on a box midway between them.

"You see us exhausted, my dear Rose," chirped Mr. Colegate. "I may call you Rose, may I not? Such a charming name —recruiting our strength before embarking on the next stage of our labors. Ah, tea! What a considerate thought! How delicious!" But Rose noticed, when she carried the cups down again, that he had hardly touched his, taken no more than a courtesy sip. Was the silence interrupted by her entry a sullen silence? An acrimonious silence? A conspiratorial silence? There had been a positive quality to it, of that Rose felt certain. And, on the Sunday, as she went about her weekend tasks and tended the children, she could not avoid the irrational notion that the Colegates, mousy-quiet themselves (they seemed to be late risers), were, as she swept, or clinked pots in the kitchen, or merely ran up and downstairs, sitting motionless, as she had first discovered them—*listening* to her.

On Sunday evening Dr. Cobb dropped in, unannounced.

"Passing by, thought I might as well. Temperatures down yet? Never mind, it has to take its course. Keep 'em in bed, though; no getting up to watch TV. That measles bug is a bad one; young Pete Finn, the vet's son, know who I mean?

Round-faced boy." She nodded. "Took pneumonia—died this morning. Couldn't get the temperature down."

"*Pete?* Pete Finn?" She was transfixed by a pang of pity and terror. "But he's such a big strong boy; we know him well. He's—was—a friend of Bob's."

Cobb shook his head. "Didn't make it. Don't tell you this to scare you—just to warn. Well—keep on with the pills. All you can do." He made for the door fast, turned to say with a touch of inquisitiveness and something else—malice?—under his good nature—"Hear you've got new lodgers." He jerked his thumb upwards. "They didn't stay in his father's house too long!"

"You know the admiral then?"

He nodded; he knew everybody. "Patient. Haven't met the younger generation though; been in foreign parts, haven't they? Good thing they left the old boy; rubbing him up the wrong way. He said they were hastening his end. Behaving themselves here, are they?"

"They seem fine—why?" She was instantly alarmed.

"Oh, nothing, nothing. Glad you found somebody. Only I did hear—" He gestured, tipping up an invisible glass.

Oh, thought Rose, that would explain the shaking hands and trouble about driving. "*Both?*" she mouthed unhappily. He shrugged.

"Only in moderation, I daresay. Could be worse. Could be heroin! Take care, now—call me at the least worry."

With a carefree slam he was into his car and away.

On Monday, a prey to hideous qualms and misgivings, Rose drove to the office of *Woman's Scene*. She had left prepared food of every kind ready to be fed to her children; a paper tacked to the wall with her phone number, the doctor's number, the plumber, electrician, hospital; typed instructions stuck on all the household appliances. For Mrs. Colegate had asked if she might use the washing machine, the iron, sewing machine, vacuum. "My father-in-law was always terribly difficult about letting us use his things," she confided.

Press week on the magazine was always a scramble of last-minute work; Rose found it impossible to leave the office before six thirty. She arrived home late and in trepidation, though Mrs. Colegate, that morning, had been wholly friendly and reassuring. (Mr. Colegate had not been visible.)

"Don't you worry about a *thing*, my dear; it will really be a pleasure to look after your nice children, dear little things."

She had seemed decidedly calmer than on the day they arrived; her hands shook less.

When Rose opened the door, her house was totally silent; and downstairs, all in darkness. She flipped a switch—no light. In panic, she ran up the stairs. Here there was darkness too, though dim lights came from the children's rooms. When she went to see Titch, Rose discovered the source of this subdued light; Mr. Colegate was there, reading *Kim* aloud to her daughter by the flicker of two candles. His high, monotonous bird-like voice—which had seemed, as she entered, mysteriously to come from somewhere up in the ceiling—ceased when he saw Rose.

Despite the dim light, he was still wearing his eyeshade.

"Ah, there you are at last, my dear," he said graciously to Rose. "Then I will retire."

"Has—has everything been all right?" Rose hoped that the nervousness and dislike in her voice were not as audible to him as they seemed to her.

"Just as right as it could be!" Mr. Colegate declared with great gaiety. He added judiciously, "But I believe your daughter is not very used to *men*—"

"My husband died when she was only three—"

"Ah, I see—That explains it. So long ago." He sighed. "Might I ask—Did your husband live here, when he was alive? In this house?"

"No, we moved here after his death."

"Ah, too bad." He seemed disappointed. "I was asking the children about him—"

He took a step, and a strong, sweetish scent, of whiskey and hair oil, was released.

Rose longed for him to be gone. She could see, what seemed to have escaped Mr. Colegate's notice, under the eyeshade and the dim light, that Titch was in a silent agony of terrified tears that might any minute reach screaming pitch.

"Well, good night, Mr. Colegate—thank you so much—" and, as he mercifully left the room, and she heard his own door shut behind him:

"My *lamb!* What's the matter?"

Titch flung herself, quivering, into her mother's arms. "He's *horrible!* I couldn't understand a *single* word he *said!* Not a word! His voice is so strange! It seemed to come from the roof. And he smells *awful.* Please don't let him come in here any more."

"No, of course I won't." With sinking heart Rose wondered how this was to be achieved without mortally offending Mr. Colegate; she suspected that he might be a very touchy man.

As soon as she could detach herself from the panic-stricken Titch, Rose went to visit Bob. Here the scene seemed calmer. Bob was sitting up in bed, flushed, but impassive, wrapped in a quilt, playing cards on a pastry board with Mrs. Colegate. Two more flickering candles lit the room.

"Your son has a natural aptitude for cards." Mrs. Colegate said, smiling, ducking out from under the sloping roof. "I've taught him Spider; and before that he learned Napoleon, Streets and Alleys, Klondyke, and The Beleaguered Castle. He learns like lightning."

"Bless him." Rose stroked the tousled fair head. "It's so kind of you. . . ." With relief she saw that Bob, though not in the best of spirits, had not been reduced to Titch's state of despair. She felt his forehead. It was very hot. He twitched away nervously from her street-cold hand.

"Why all the candles?" Rose asked. "Did the main fuse blow?"

"I can't say," Mrs. Colegate looked vague. "Something went

wrong. But, anyway, my husband and I really prefer candle-light."

Rose did not. In a Tudor house, largely constructed of timber and lath, candles were too great a fire hazard, and she groped her way down to the cellar and mended the three separate fuses that seemed to have blown. However, even after the rest of the rooms were blazing with light, she noticed (when outside fetching her briefcase from the car) that only a dim flicker still emanated from the Colegates' windows. I hope to God they've straightened up all that clutter, she thought apprehensively; she could hardly forbid the Colegates to use candles if such was their preference, but it did seem risky with all those obstacles on the floor to trip them. Perhaps they were straight by now, though.

Later on in the evening she was obliged to visit their room. The phone rang: it was a male voice asking for Mr. Desmond Colegate.

"What name shall I say?" inquired Rose.

"Hugh Morgan-Sleigh—Admiral Colegate's solicitor. I have been trying this number all day!" said the voice irritably.

"I'll see if they are in; but I rather believe I heard them go out half an hour ago," said Rose.

As she gulped down her late, hasty supper, she had heard footsteps and mutterings on the stairs.

Pondering, she tapped on the Colegates' door. Twice during the day she had tried to phone home in order to ask after the children but had got no reply on either occasion.

Were the Colegates telephone-shy?

The tapping produced no response, and she cautiously opened the door, automatically switching on the light. Something scurried hastily in a corner, she caught a glimpse of a smallish, whitish creature which vanished under a corner of blanket hanging from the divan.

The Colegates were nowhere to be seen. And the rooms were still just as untidy as they had been four days ago. A guttering candle leaned precariously over the edge of a saucer. Rose extinguished it and went back to the phone.

"They must be out, I'm afraid. Shall I leave them a message to call you?"

"*That* won't be any use," he said sourly. "I suppose I shall have to come and see them to explain the Admiral's intentions." He sounded as if he found the prospect intensely disagreeable.

"You might catch them at friends—if you had any idea where to phone?" Rose suggested.

"More likely in a pub," he muttered, to himself, not Rose, and hung up.

She had intended to wait up in order to tell them about the call and also ask about the creature—*what* could it have been? a ferret? a lizard? a coypu?—but they returned home so extremely late that by the time they came in she had given up and, exhausted, retired to bed. She slept lightly, though, and heard their shuffling feet on the stairs after the church clock struck one. Not a pub then; Mr. Morgan-Sleigh must have been wrong about that.

In the morning there was no sound from the Colegate area. Not daring to leave the children—both running fevers—without being certain that somebody was alert enough to attend to their needs, Rose waited as long as possible, then tapped at the door. A very long silence ensued. Rose tapped again. A drowsy voice called, "Who is it?"

"It's me—Rose. I'm sorry to disturb you—"

After another long pause Mrs. Colegate came flapping to the door in a faded silk wrapper that must once have been memorably ornate. Her face was chalk-pale, her hands shook wildly.

Rose passed on the lawyer's message—which Mrs. Colegate received without expression—and then added, "I'm sorry to bother you"—why did she keep saying that, it wasn't true—"but I've just phoned the doctor, and he says, if the children's temperatures aren't down by noon, get in touch with him and

he'll come round. Just phone him and he'll come," she repeated, as Mrs. Colegate continued to look unreceptive.

"Phone the doctor . . . ? Oh, I won't do that, I'll run round
to his office," Mrs. Colegate said after a pause. "I've seen it, it's
in the square, isn't it?"

"Yes," said Rose, rather astonished. "But you'd much better
phone. He won't be there, he'll be on his rounds—they'll have
to find him."

"I'll go," repeated Mrs. Colegate. "I like the fresh air."

"You won't forget, will you?" There was something so odd
about the woman that Rose was deeply troubled at having to
leave the children in her charge. She went on, "I don't like to
seem like a silly, fussing parent, but since the news about poor
little Peter Finn's death—"

"Peter Finn's death?" Mrs. Colegate looked a little more intelligent. "The vet's boy at South Dean? Such a sweet boy—he
used to wash our car and my husband taught him to play
cribbage—"

Mention of the vet reminded Rose of something. "By the
way—do you have a pet? When I looked in last night I thought
I saw—The thing is, I hadn't really reckoned—The house isn't
very big—"

For several moments Mrs. Colegate remained quite silent,
her face noncommittal. Then, as if after reflection, she said,
"A pet?"

"I thought, when I went up about the phone call I saw
something like a ferret—"

"Oh, you mean my sister's Chinese rabbit?" Mrs. Colegate
said, as if suddenly enlightened. "Don't worry, I'll take it back
to her today." And she added, "*We* don't like pets at all. Don't
worry," she finished absently.

Rose nodded, left the house, and ran to her car. She was
very late. And it was beginning to snow.

On both the following evenings the fuses were all blown
when Rose arrived home. Some activity of the Colegates apparently put an excessive strain on the wiring. Mending the

fuses, Rose resolved to ask them about it when she had a little more time—but there were so many things on her mind as well. The children's still soaring temperatures, the unsorted mess in the Colegates' rooms, visible whenever they briefly left the door open—ought Rose to help them tidy it?—the intermittent snow, which made driving a terror to Rose, never confident in a car at the best of times—the hectic going-to-press nonstop action at the magazine.

Then, on Wednesday evening, there came a call from the police.

"Mrs. Burdock? Sar'n't Grimbold here. I believe you have a Mr. Colegate staying with you who owns a white Cortina, registration DDR 01 439J? Would you mind telling him that he's parked it illegally in Mary Lane and unless it's removed within half an hour it will be towed away at his expense?"

"Oh yes—I'll tell him—very kind of you to tip him off," Rose said to Sergeant Grimbold, who was an old friend, and he said:

"Confidentially, they keep leaving their car in all sorts of crazy places. You'd better warn them or they're in for trouble."

"Oh, good *heavens!*" said Mr. Colegate irritably when Rose relayed the message to him, somewhat watered down. "I must say, it is a *great* pity we are not permitted to put our car in the graveyard next door. There would be *plenty* of room among the graves. This town is so awkward and confusing at night, as the streets are so poorly lit." Ironic that he, with his preference for candlelight, should complain of that, Rose thought. He went on, "Quite often, in the morning, other people have parked so inconsiderately that it is almost impossible for us to locate our car. My poor wife had to spend *several hours* today searching for it."

This explained Bob's complaint. "We didn't get our lunch today till four, Mom. Need these Colegates stay? I don't really like them."

"Oh, dear, love. Nor do I, much. But they *are* keeping an eye on you. And they've paid a month's rent in advance. What don't you like about them?"

"Everything! And his puppets are the absolute *end!*"

"Puppets?"

"He makes them out of china or something. They clink. He showed me a couple this afternoon when we were playing cards. One moved by itself—horrible! We played canasta, and he said if I won I could have one of the smaller puppets. But I wouldn't want one; they give me the creeps. Anyway I didn't win."

On Thursday morning, early, Mrs. Joubert sent for Rose. The magazine had been safely put to bed; there was time to draw breath. Rose hurried to the editor's office wondering what fault or omission of hers had come under scrutiny; she could think of several possibilities in the last few desperate days.

But this summons was of a personal nature. Mrs. Joubert came to the point directly.

"I've been talking to my housekeeper at South Dean—she tells me she heard the young Colegates had rented rooms in your house."

Young Colegates? Rose would hardly have classified them as that, but she supposed that, compared with the Admiral in his late eighties, they rated as young.

"Yes, that's right."

"Well, *get them out at once!* You *can't* let them stay in your house."

"But—but—" Rose stammered, utterly taken aback, "they gave *you* as a reference! That—that was why I let them come—"

"Like their impudence. They'd no right to," Mrs. Joubert said incisively. "My dear, they nearly drove that wretched old man mad! He said they were hurrying him toward his end. They are an appalling couple!"

"What's the matter with them?"

"Well, they drink like fishes for a start. But there are much worse things—they have all kinds of murky habits—you have *got* to get rid of them!"

"But they've paid a month's rent!"

"Pay it back. Get them out."

"How can I possibly do that?"

"Invent something. Say you've got your mother-in-law coming to live with you. I'm serious."

"But—they are looking after my children who have mumps and measles."

Rose felt herself close to fainting with sheer despair.

"You'll just have to take some time off," Mrs. Joubert said impatiently. "Lucky we've just gone to press. . . ."

In a small, detached, ironic corner of her mind, Rose wondered if the time off would have been granted otherwise.

"Don't come in till next Monday. Tell them some story—fix *something*. Okay? And you'd better leave early today."

Nonetheless there was much clearing up to do after the scrambled press day. The January afternoon was darkening by the time Rose parked the Mini opposite her front door. The sight of Dr. Cobb's car arrogantly straddling the double yellow lines across the road turned her cold with apprehension.

"I'm afraid the lad's coming down with measles too," the doctor told her, outside Bob's door. "This is going to be the really tricky time. . . . I've left a new lot of medicine for him to take. Try an ice pack. And lots of fluids. I'll be back later this evening."

"You don't think he should go into the hospital?" Rose tried to keep her voice level.

"My dear, they're packed to the gills. Still—don't worry. See you later."

Don't worry, Rose thought, pressing both hands against her aching temples.

Ten minutes afterwards, as she ran up the stairs with a jug of barley water, she found her way impeded by Mr. Colegate, fatly occupying most of the narrow landing.

"I'm taking these in to amuse him," he chirped gaily.

She was too exhausted to pretend.

"No, he doesn't want anything like that, Mr. Colegate. He's far too sick."

Yet there was something rather repulsively fascinating about Mr. Colegate's puppets, which he held dangling from either hand. China, Bob had said, and she had thought he must be mistaken, but in fact the puppets were made of ceramic—a series of bell-shaped pottery pieces, a large one for the body, with painted face, and smaller ones for the arms and legs, each slotting into the one above, threaded on leather thongs. They clinked slightly as they moved. The faces, though depicted by no more than half a dozen strokes of black and white paint, wore such expressions of malign hostility that it was easy to see why they had upset Bob. Thank heaven Titch had not seen them.

"He's too sick," Rose repeated firmly.

"Poor boy," Mr. Colegate sighed. "It's hard—when one is young—to be so very ill. You're sure I couldn't show him just *one* puppet? I have a big one—bigger than these—which moves all by itself; I've trained it to do that. He liked that one."

"No thanks, Mr. Colegate."

Mrs. Colegate opened their door and put her face round. She looked fatigued and frightened. For a moment Rose thought she could hear a faint, high-pitched crying coming from the room behind her. Then she stepped out and closed the door.

"Ventriloquism," said her husband. "Did you know I could throw my voice, my dear Rose?"

He twitched his face, and a squeaky voice came from among the rafters up above them.

"*Let me out, let me out!*"

"*Don't* do that, Desmond," said his wife hastily. "Tell me, where did you put the collecting bottle? I need it for—"

"I am trying to divert our dear Rose, Laura."

"Well, she isn't amused. Where did you leave the bottle?"

"I daresay it is in the car," he replied pettishly.

"Where's the car?"

"God knows if *you* don't!" he snapped and went into their room, slamming the door. For the instant that it was open, Rose thought she heard the crying again. Then there was a thump and silence. Am I going mad? she wondered, carrying the barley water in to Bob. He was slightly delirious and pushed her away crying, "Don't you let them near me or I'll smash them!"

Titch, too, was worse that evening and complained of pains all around her neck. But she would still take fruit juice, which Bob refused. Rose, squeezing oranges in her kitchen, was interrupted by Mr. Colegate, who seemed aggrieved.

"I am very *fond* of your children," he announced aggressively.

"That's kind of you, Mr. Colegate. . . . I'm sure you are."

"Then why does your daughter scream like a maniac when I go into her room?"

"She's very sick. She's only eight. She's not used to men."

"She's used to the doctor."

"That's different. She's known him for years."

"I would like to teach her how to play clock patience. *Any* child her age can learn that."

"Mr. Colegate, I would rather you didn't go into her room, just at present."

He looked at Rose loweringly, but at this moment his wife came in, flustered, brushing snowflakes off her shabby head-scarf.

"Desmond, I can't *find* the car. Can't you remember where we left it last?"

"*You* were driving."

"No I wasn't—" she began, but he dragged her sharply out into the passage.

Rose heard them squabbling.

"You *must* remember." "Well, I don't." "You *were* driving." "Shut up! Try to think where you put it." "I didn't put it *any*where." "I've looked all over the town. If we don't find the bottle soon it'll be—they're getting fractious." "*I* don't hear anything." "That's because you're deaf, Desmond."

He *was* a bit deaf, Rose had noticed; often she had to repeat things she said to him.

"Did you try in the alley next to the library—where it says 'Librarian Only'?"

"No, I didn't."

"I think it might be there; go and see."

"You go and quiet them down, then; put them in the bird-cage."

When the Colegates had departed, Rose took Titch her orange juice. She thought she could hear a kind of scuffle taking place in the Colegates' room, mixed with subdued curses.

Just as she was carrying the empty mug downstairs again, Mrs. Colegate came in through the front door. Evidently her quest this time had been successful; she bore a heavy-looking gallon-sized flagon made of black glass. It was encased in a sort of basketwork which was covered all over with beads—black, green, blue, red, and white. The beading formed letters, which ran crisscross, up, down, and sideways, like a crossword puzzle; in her brief glimpse Rose saw no words she recognized, but noticed the letters O, A, T, N, E, and S. It was an extremely foreign-looking article; perhaps the Colegates had brought it back with them from Tehran. What could they keep in it that was required with such urgency? Although the black glass looked massively thick, the frail Mrs. Colegate appeared to be able to carry it without too much difficulty, as if the contents were light. It could be oxygen, thought Rose. Or crushed laurel leaves for killing moths—why did they call it a collecting bottle?

She went upstairs again to read aloud to Titch, who complained that she ached all over.

The crying from the Colegates' room had ceased. Rose decided that she had imagined it.

Dr. Cobb came back at eleven and said that Bob was holding his own.

"You get a bit of sleep now and have a look at him around two. Call me if you're at all bothered," he said. "Try to sleep a little now."

"Okay. You're very good," Rose muttered.

The Colegates, according to evening custom, had gone out. Rose suppressed an urge to bolt the front door so that they could not get back in. She could not resist the temptation to peep into their room. The floor was still covered with things. The plastic garment bag hung from a rafter, swaying slightly. Near the door stood the large birdcage, covered by a square of red baize. Gingerly, Rose twitched the baize up—and let it drop again with a shudder of disgust. On the floor of the cage were three smallish, whittish wrinkled things, huddled to-gether motionless: what could they have been? They resem-bled embryos with horrible little tapering, attenuated limbs. They reminded her vaguely of William Blake's paintings. They couldn't have been alive; they couldn't have been real, she told herself. It was just a pile of chamois leather or some-thing like that. Bits of crumpled plastic perhaps.

Tomorrow she would give the Colegates notice to go. The first thing in the morning. As soon as she saw them.

Trembling, she shut the door again, went to her own room, set the alarm for two A.M., and fell on the bed fully clothed. She had thought she would never go to sleep, but she went off instantly, as if she had swallowed a knockout dose, and imme-diately began to dream.

She dreamed that she was watching Desmond Colegate and her son play cards. The cards were laid out like gravestones all over a flat board, and the room was lit by two candles, one black, one white. Mr. Colegate pointed to the candles and said, "You remember what the Egyptians believed. We are split into ten parts, of which this is the kha, or double, and that the khu, or spirit. Are you paying attention, boy?"

"Yes," Bob said sleepily—he was lolling back on the pillow, hardly able to keep his eyes open.

"Very well: we shall play Devil's Bedposts," Colegate said,

and he began moving the cards into a square formation. "The winner takes both candles—right?"

"Don't play with him, Bob!" Rose wanted to scream, but her voiced remained trapped inside; her lips would not open.

The players began moving the cards about, murmuring incomprehensible terms. "I buy the devil." "I cross the equator." "Cold hand takes the tiger." "Go now!" "Queen of the night takes ten."

Suddenly Colegate slapped all his cards down on the board, shouting.

"Dead Hand! I win!"

And, picking up a black conical candle extinguisher, he snuffed out both flames and put the candles in his pocket.

Rose thought she had woken herself by shrieking, but found that it was the shrilling alarm in her ear that had roused her. She stumbled out of bed and quietly opened her bedroom door.

On the landing she was dismayed to see Desmond Colegate, also fully clothed. He seemed to be coming from Bob's room and was carrying a flashlight which cast a small round pool of light before him on the floor. He did not observe Rose; he opened his own door and exclaimed in a harsh whisper:

"Laura. *Laura!* The little brute got away. Where did you leave the bottle?"

Her sleepy voice answered, ". . . It's back in the car."

"Where's the bloody car?"

"Don't you remember? You left it in the graveyard."

He spun round, and Rose heard the thump of his feet down the stairs and the soft slam of the front door. Aghast, she stepped to the landing window, which also looked out on to the graveyard, thrust back the curtain, and saw, in bright moonlight, against the snow, the Colegates' car drawn up askew just inside the gate. She was in time to see Colegate: he held the wicker-wrapped flask in one hand, what looked like a white towel in the other; he was dashing about among the gravestones, apparently in pursuit of some elusive and darting quarry. He made frantic flaps and lunges with the cloth, blundered into the stone slabs, tripped, picked himself up again, and stumbled on.

But presently, dropping the bottle, he pressed both hands violently against his breastbone, as if coughing or choking—stood in this position, anchored, for several moments—then fell, heavily, onto the snow, and lay still.

Rose heard a shallow breathing behind her and turned to see Laura Colegate looking past her shoulder.

"What is it, what *is* it?" she muttered apprehensively, pushing aside her dangling hair with tremulous hands.

"Your husband is out in the graveyard, Mrs. Colegate," said Rose bleakly. "I think you had better go to him; he seems to have been taken ill."

Whimpering in distress, the other woman shuffled down the stairs. "Desmond. Desmond, why couldn't you wait for me?" she called plaintively, and the door slammed behind her. Rose waited a moment, saw her approach her husband's body, stoop, and recoil with upflung hands, glancing suspiciously round her as if expecting crowds of onlookers.

Rose turned and ran to her son's room. His window stood wide open. A scatter of cards lay over the quilt. Bob was sprawled in the bed motionless, with his face to the wall. Rose, trying to keep her fingers steady on his wrist, could find no pulse. She ran down the stairs to the telephone.

"Mom? I'm thirsty!" came a feeble croak from Titch's room.

"Just a minute, love, shan't be long."

Rose began dialing the doctor's number; as she did so, she heard the front door close, and Mrs. Colegate's dragging steps cross the front hall.

Listening

He had been walking up Fifth Avenue for about ten minutes when the cat fell. He had been walking along, minding his own business, not looking about him—though it was a beautiful day, the first of spring, with a warm, keen wind ruffling the vapor trails in the sky and dislodging the pigeons from cornices where they sat sunning. He was preoccupied, to tell the truth, worrying over what he could ever find to say about Mrs. Schaber's lesson, which he was on his way to observe.

Listening, she taught. "What in God's name is *listening?*" he had asked Mark Calvert, who worked in the same department. "Oh, it's a form of musical appreciation—little Schaber's a bit of a nut, but she's quite a fine musician, too, in her way." He had not even met her, so far as he was aware—she was just another of the two-hundred-odd faceless names on the college faculty list. So now he had to give up his free day, this beautiful mild, melting, burgeoning day, to go and invigilate her class and decide whether she would be worthy of tenure, on the basis of whether or not she was able to teach kids to listen. Is there a craft about listening—an art that has to be learned? —he wondered. Don't we begin listening from the very moment we are born?

At that moment the cat hit. He was approaching the Twenty-eighth Street intersection when he heard this horribly distinctive sound—a loud, solid smack, accompanied by a faint, sharp cry; indeed he had *seen* it also, he must have seen about the last six inches of its fall, as he glanced up from his moody stride, and so was able to verify that cats do *not* always land on their feet—this poor beast, which must have come from about twenty floors up, landed flat on its side and then lay twitching. Its eyes were open, but it must, please heaven, be on the point of death—ought he to *do* something about it? What *could* one do?

In no time a small crowd had collected.

"It fell from *way* up there," a woman kept saying hysterically. "I saw the whole thing—I was just crossing the street—"

"Do you think we should take it to a vet?" someone suggested.

"Oh, what's the use? The poor thing's dying anyway."

"Tell the super in the block? That looks like a valuable cat—"

"Lucky it didn't land on somebody—could probably kill a person—"

As they discussed it, the cat twitched again. Its eyes closed definitively.

"Oh, its poor owner. She'll wonder what *happened* to it—"

"Shouldn't have left her window open if you ask *me*—"

He left them and walked on. He was going to be late if he didn't hurry. It *had* looked like a valuable cat. Its fur was a rich mixture of browns and creams in which dark chocolate predominated, its eyes a wild fanatic blue. It seemed to belong to the luxury class, along with costly monogrammed luggage, gold accessories and jeweled watches: objects of conspicuous expenditure. And yet, poor thing, it had been alive, had its own nature—that faint piteous cry still hung in his ears, an expostulation against undeserved agony.

He *had* seen Mrs. Schaber before, it turned out; he recognized her as soon as he entered the classroom. She was the odd little woman whom he had passed one day in the main lobby while she was deep in conversation with a deaf student. He had been much struck by her at the time, two or three months back. She was quite short, only about five foot, with her dark hair coiled

in a bun low on her neck. She wore jeans, a flannel shirt, a
sweater tied by the arms around her waist, espadrilles; she
looked like a student. But her face was that of a woman in her
mid-forties—somewhat lined, especially around the mouth.
Her eyes were large, brownish green, almond shaped, set wide
apart; and her face was long and oval, with a particularly long
jaw and upper lip, and a lower lip that extended, sometimes,
above the upper one, giving her a look of comical pugnacity.
But what had attracted his attention on that occasion was the
extreme vivacity of her face—dozens of expressions chased
each other across it: sympathetic, hilarious, grave, intent, sor-
rowful, ecstatic, ferocious—while her hands, meanwhile,
twinkled away with unbelievable speed, flicking their sound-
less message to the student she was addressing.

"Is *she* deaf, too?" he had asked Charlie Whitney, with whom
he had been talking on that occasion.

"Schaber? Lord, no! She can hear *and* talk the hind leg off a
mule!"

She was doing so now, addressing her students in a flood of
loquacity. But she broke off to greet him with a rather con-
stricted smile.

"Oh—Professor Middlemass—good morning! Would you
like to sit here? Or would you rather walk about? Please do
just what you want—make yourself at home! I was—I was
beginning to explain to the students that this morning I am
going to play them tapes recorded on my trip to Europe and
Africa last year. I shall analyze the background of each tape
before I play it. Then, later in the lesson, I shall demonstrate
the relation of the sounds they have heard to musical patterns
and structures and explain how this in its turn demonstrates
the relevance of music to language."

Nodding vaguely—she had rattled this out so fast that he
hardly took in her meaning—he settled down to listen, observ-
ing that eighteen out of her nineteen students were present,
and that they were watching her with expressions that ranged
from indulgent amusement through skepticism and mild bore-

dom to absorbed devotion. Only one boy looked wholly bored: he was stretched back in his seat with his blond hair over his eyes, his hands in his pockets, his legs stuck out in front, his head bowed forward: he appeared to be studying his shoelaces through the strands of his hair.

The tapes, when Mrs. Schaber began to play them, were a bit of a surprise: they were so extremely quiet. She had been allotted a soundproof music studio for her demonstration, and this was just as well, for some of the sounds were just barely audible. "Now, this is the Camargue: you can hear grasses rustling and, very far off, the noise of the sea. And after five minutes you will notice a faint drumming in the distance. That is the sound of hooves: the wild horses. They never come very close; you will have to listen carefully.

"Now this recording was taken in Denmark, in the bog country: you can hear reeds and dry rushes; the sound is not dissimilar to the tape of the Camargue that I played you earlier, but this one was taken *inland*; there was a different quality to the air; it was less resonant. Also, after three minutes of tape, you will hear a stork shifting about in its nest; I was standing close to a cottage that had a stork's nest on its roof."

Mrs. Schaber went on to describe in some detail what materials storks used in building their nests and then played her tape. As she listened to it herself, her face wore a recollecting, tranquil, amused expression.

Gradually, while the lesson proceeded, Middlemass observed how the students were becoming polarized by her exposition. The ones who had looked indulgent or bored at the start were now gazing drearily at the ceiling, picking their noses or their teeth, chewing gum, manifesting exasperation and tedium; others were watching Mrs. Schaber with fanatical attention. The blond boy still stared at his feet.

Toward the end of her batch of tapes came some that had been recorded in the Congo rain forest. Middlemass had always been fascinated by the thought of the jungle, ever since reading Duguid's *Green Hell*; he had not the least intention of ever walking into a jungle himself, but he occasionally liked to imagine doing so. Now he listened with careful interest to the rich silences, the ticking, cheeping, chirring, shrilling, buzzing, scraping sibilances that Mrs. Schaber had collected; for the first time he began to feel some groping acceptance of what she was proffering. He noticed, also, that the blond boy had taken his hands out of his pockets and had his head cocked in an attitude of acute attention.

During the second half of the lesson, Mrs. Schaber proceeded to play short snatches of music and demonstrate their resemblance to vocal patterns and to some of the natural sounds that she had presented earlier. This, Middlemass thought, was really interesting; the whole lesson began to cohere for him, and he changed his mind about what he would say in his report, which, half-phrased in his head already, had not been particularly enthusiastic. "Too divorced from reality —students did not seem very engaged—Mrs. Schaber has a gift, but it seems devoted to inessentials—" Now he resolved to say something more favorable.

At this point there came an interruption to the lesson. A secretary tapped at the door to say that Mrs. Schaber was wanted in the main office. "The police have just called up from your home, Mrs. Schaber; I'm afraid your apartment has been broken into, and they want you to go home and say what has been taken."

"Oh my god!" The poor little woman looked utterly stricken; her expressive face changed to a Greek mask of tragedy, mouth wide open, eyes dilated.

"Shall I go with you to the office?" Middlemass offered, touched by compassion because he had been filled with rather disparaging thoughts about her during the first half of her lesson and because she did seem as if she had sustained a mortal blow. The blond boy had already risen to his feet, moved compactly forward, and taken her arm. But Middlemass accompanied them anyway; he felt the need somehow to demonstrate his friendly feeling and sympathy.

While Mrs. Schaber talked on the phone in the secretary's room, it became plain that matters were even worse than she had feared.

"Oh no, not all my *tapes?*" she cried out. "What could they want those for? Smashed—wrecked—oh, *no!*"— pressing her clenched fist against her thin chest as if she were trying, forcibly, to push her anguished, expanded heart back into position. Wordlessly, the secretary went to fetch her a cup of coffee. The blond boy stood silent with his eyes fixed on her face. When she had laid the receiver back in its rest and was staring across the room, quite dazed, with fixed, sightless eyes, Middlemass asked her gently:

"Is it very bad?"

"They have taken a whole *lot* of stuff," she muttered, "and all the rest they have destroyed—smashed up. Everything—"

Inattentively, she gulped at the coffee the secretary handed her.

"I keep wondering whether I forgot to lock the door—when I went out this morning—the super found it open, that was why he phoned the police—I was so nervous—in a hurry—*did* I forget to lock it?"

"Oh, no!" Middlemass exclaimed, horrified. "You don't mean to say that you were nervous because of *me*—because your lesson was going to be observed—that on account of *that* you might have forgotten to lock up—?"

He could not bear the idea that he might in any way be instrumental in her catastrophe.

"Of *course* I was nervous!" she said. "Naturally I was nervous! Excuse me—they want me right away—I must go back to the classroom and collect my things—"

"I am most terribly sorry this has happened," he said, following her back along the corridor, wondering if his words were getting through to her at all. "I had been enjoying your lesson so much—it seemed to me one of the most interesting and original discourses that I have ever listened to—"

In his own ears, his voice sounded horribly forced and insincere. He wondered if *that* was one of the things he had learned from her lesson. How to detect the falsity in human utterance? And yet what he had said was the truth—*meant* to be the truth, he told himself. He noticed the blond boy's eyes on him, assessing, skeptical.

"I'm going to give you a very good report," he told poor Mrs. Schaber, as she began collecting her gear in the classroom. "If that helps to cheer you up at all—"

"Well—thank you—of course it does," she answered distractedly, shoveling tapes into a big worn woolen bag, filled already with a mass of untidy odds and ends. It was evident that she heard him only with a single thread of attention; the rest of her mind was elsewhere. "It's like having lost a whole continent, a whole *world*," she murmured. "Years and years of work."

"Well, you've still got the Congo forest, because you had it here," the blond boy reminded her, and at that she suddenly gave him her flashing urchin grin, thrusting forward the long lower jaw and lower lip, nodding her head up and down.

"That's true! One forest left—perhaps it will seed itself. But there's not all that amount of *time* left."

When Mrs. Schaber had gone, Middlemass walked out of the college. He felt too disturbed to want to eat in the cafeteria and talk to colleagues; he wanted a long period of time and solitude to settle his feelings. Poor little woman, so stricken and bereft—he thought of her returning to her wrecked apartment, like a bird to a robbed nest. And the worst of it was the anxiety as to whether it had been her own carelessness that had invited the thieves; he knew how such an idea would haunt *him*, if he had been the victim. He imagined her trying and trying again to resurrect the process of her departure in the morning, to discover whether she had in fact left the door unlocked—had she taken the key out of her purse, had she put it back—as if it could make any real difference to the disaster itself.

Walking along Fifty-seventh Street, Middlemass tried to

calm his mind by wandering into a number of art galleries, at
random, looking first at a show of nineteenth-century portrait
photographs, then at some watercolor landscapes, then some
classic Matisses, magically soothing, then some semiabstract
sculpture, recognizable articles broken into fragments and re-
united into strange disjointed forms—then a show of cartoons
—a collection of Japanese prints—one of book illustrations
from the 'nineties. He was moving westwards all the time; he
thought he would presently buy a sandwich and eat it in the
park. The day was still idyllically fine and warm.

In a small room adjoining the exhibition of book illustrations there was a show by a minor artist whose name was
unknown to him; the title of the exhibition was simply "Collages." Through the open door he caught a glimpse of quiet,
restful black and white forms. He stepped inside, meaning to
give the show a quick two minutes and then go in search of his
sandwich.

The collages, contained inside plain wood frames, were
made up from all kinds of materials—fabrics, press cuttings,
bits of wood, of metal, of oilcloth, tar cloth, wire netting,
string, bent wire, gauze, clay, foam rubber—all dyed or
stained either black or white. They had been assembled,
molded, pressed, organized into shapes that were vaguely human, vaguely monstrous in outline: straining bodies were suggested, extended limbs, odd movements of exuberant dance, of
cowering terror, of sad, limp resignation. The titles, on labels
beside the frames, were all single words: Waiting; Fearing;
Hoping; Expecting; Exulting.

Despite a general feeling of slight distaste for what he considered rather pretentious, facile stuff, without the merit of
true creativity, Middlemass found himself oddly struck by
these forms—they seemed to touch on some nerve in him that
was not normally affected but had, perhaps, been bruised already that day. He walked slowly around the room, considering the occupant of each frame in turn—as if they had been
creatures in cages, he told himself.

Returning, finally, toward the door, he looked at the last frame, which had the title "Begging." A crippled, bandaged creature crouched, huddled, in the middle of the frame; its head, composed of wire netting, seemed to be swathed in wrappings and gave the impression of blind, listening urgency. One of its limbs, a bent pipe wrapped in tarred rag, extended, pleadingly, right out of the frame, and was flattened at the extremity into the approximate form of a hand; to this hand a small white square of paper in the shape of a visiting card had been fastened by staples.

Moving closer, to discover whether the tiny characters on the card were real letters, real words, he received a shock. Neatly printed across the white, in black India ink, he read his own name: JOHN MIDDLEMASS, M.D.

He gasped and then laughed. Turning to the girl at the desk, in an attempt to cover the extraordinary agitation he felt at this strange, this outrageous portent, he said:

"What an amazing thing! The name—this name here, in the picture—on the card—it's *my* name, John Middlemass!—Only I am not a doctor," he added.

"Is that so?" The girl—thin, dark, long-haired, wan—looked at him with a wholly uninterested, lackluster indifference which immediately seemed to reduce the coincidence to minimal proportions. After all, her look suggested, *somebody* in the whole of New York has to have that name—what's so peculiar about *your* having it? Why are you making such a to-do? "Perhaps that artist got it out of the phone book," she suggested, yawning. "But you're not a doctor, you say?" she added kindly, as if to humor him.

"No, no, I'm a teacher—" Feeling foolish, as if he had made a fuss about nothing at all, he left the gallery and went to buy his sandwich. Bacon, lettuce, and tomato. Then he walked up Madison Avenue, feeling the sun warm on his shoulder blades, and turned left, toward the park. He could hear sparrows chirping and one shrill bird cry, far in the distance, that took him back in memory to a spring holiday on Cape Cod.

The day was so warm that all the park benches were filled. Finally, unable to find a seat on one, he settled on a slope of warm rock near the pond, looking south toward the Plaza Hotel. The water in the pond was low, and patches of reeds stood out on small mud islands; as he ate his sandwich, he noticed how neatly gulls landed on the surface of the water to swim and drink and preen themselves and how clumsily pigeons, unable to land on the water, thumped down on an island of rock and then waddled to the edge in order to drink. Planes droned overhead, and helicopters stuttered; an ambulance siren wailed and gibbered not far off on its way across town.

Presently Middlemass began to be aware of the couple who sat on the end of the bench nearest him, a girl and a boy, intent on their conversation with each other. It was not so much the human pair he noticed as their animals. The boy had a dog, which he allowed to roam loose: a kind of black mongrel with traces of retriever, a loose-jointed, floppy, active dog that went on forays, dashing off splashily round the verge of the pond, and returned every now and again, damp, smiling, panting, to lavish affection on its master.

But the girl had a cat; making the second cat I've seen today, thought Middlemass with a sudden shiver, remembering his earlier horrible experience. What a strange day it had been! But that was how life piled up in the city, one event splashing on top of another like lava from a volcanic eruption, hardly time to assimilate an experience before the next one came tumbling about you.

This cat, though, the cat in the park, was a very different creature from that poor dead, expensive, elegant piece of fur that had no doubt long since been shoveled off the sidewalk and into some garbage can. This cat in the park was half white, half ginger in color. It was an old cat; its fur was patchy, molting, dusty; its ears were tattered, its nose was scarred, its tail looked moth-eaten. The girl had it on a leash, but she was paying no attention to it, and while she talked to her boyfriend the cat sulked, squatting behind the bench on which the pair sat, with its head thrust forward, as if it found the whole park, the dusty ground, the beaten-up grass, the muddy pond, the dingy sparrows, hopelessly distasteful, as if it were fed up with the world and its own ancient disheveled body.

Every now and then the black dog, returning from one of its excursions, would suddenly, with a kind of delighted surprise, rediscover the sulky cat and would then roll it over and over, tousling and biting it, rubbing its fur in the dust. The cat retaliated with what seemed a kind of resigned rage, spitting and kicking, tail bushed out, ears flattened.

"*Don't* do that, Buster," the boy would call absently, and the girl would say, "Oh, it's all right, never mind, Ginger quite enjoys it really," a statement which Middlemass, watching, considered to be quite patently untrue; it seemed to him that the cat disliked the dog's teasing roughness to the whole of its capacity for feeling.

Presently the couple rose to walk away. The dog instantly darted off ahead, delighted to be on the move again; but the cat, as if obstinately determined not to cooperate in any way during this disagreeable outing, now refused to budge. Before, it had sat sulkily ignoring its surroundings; now it wished to delay and sniff round the legs of the bench. The girl, impatient to be gone, jerked crossly at its lead, and, when it still would not follow, dragged it up bodily by the leash so that it hung in its collar, choking and scowling.

"*Don't* do that to the cat," Middlemass wanted to call out. "Pick it up properly!" But rage choked him, quite as much as its collar was choking the cat. When the girl put it down it did slowly begin to follow, trotting a few steps, then stopping to sniff things at the side of the path; its pace was not nearly fast enough to satisfy its mistress, who several times either dragged it along bodily, sliding on its feet, or again hoisted it up on the end of the leash. Middlemass felt an intense relief when the couple had passed out of view. He hated that girl; he really loathed her—But the cat was an old one, he told himself;

it must have become used to such treatment years ago—No, it was no use; how *could* the horrible girl be so insensitive to the feelings of the creature she lived with?

His hands were clenched so tightly that the knuckles, when he finally relaxed them, felt swollen and quite painful. He looked down at his hands, thinking ruefully, not so elastic as they used to be. I am growing old. I should have interfered. Why didn't I? Because if I had, the girl would only have thought that I was a meddlesome old busybody. "Mind your own business, Mister," she would have said. "This cat belongs to me and I can do what I like with it."

Interfering gets you nowhere. And where does noninterfering get you?

The day had clouded and cooled. He walked over to Fifth Avenue to catch a bus home, thinking about the various disagreeable tasks that awaited him: tax forms to be filled out, bills to be paid, household articles to be repaired, business letters to be written. However inconspicuously we endeavor to conduct our lives, creeping along, keeping our heads well down out of the line of fire, still in the end we fall prey to circumstances, he thought, and I suppose the final knockout is not one single blow, so much as a whole series of minor assaults, to which, in the end, we wearily succumb.

I'd just as soon be nibbled to death by ducks, he remembered somebody saying; where in the world could that extraordinary phrase have come from?

His bus drew to a stop, and he climbed on to it and walked along the aisle, hoping for a seat in the back row, so that he need not travel sitting sideways, which he disliked. My life, he thought, is assembled out of an endless procession of unimportant choices.

The back row was all occupied, so he took the last of the side seats, in hopes that presently somebody might get off, and then he could switch seats. The bus had a long way to go, all down Fifth Avenue. As it slowly jerked and clanked through the heavy afternoon traffic, his mind went back to Mrs.

Schaber; poor woman, she would be at home now, examining
her wrecked possessions, listening to the callous comments of
the police, who, as Middlemass knew from experience, never
offered the slightest hope of getting back any of the lost prop-
erty. They were not interested in that; the only thing that
concerned them at all was the possibility of identifying the
thieves.

"It's like losing a whole *world*," she had moaned.

But at least, thought Middlemass, she had a world to lose.

At Twenty-eighth Street he suddenly thought of the cat—
the first cat. It must have happened just about here. You'd
never guess it now. People were darting to and fro on the
pavement at that point, with their usual manic speed. The
patch of blood would have been sanded over and swept away.
So we come; so we go. What had made him think of the cat?
Before that his mind had been on Mrs. Schaber and her loss.

Then he heard the sound again: a faint, querulous grumbling mew; the sigh of meow let out by a cat who is shut up,
bored, exasperated, wishing to remind its owner of the tedium
of its plight: a kvetch in cat language.

For a moment Middlemass wondered if perhaps he might be
going mad; haunted by the ghost of a cat; of two cats. But
then, turning his head slightly, he saw that the girl close beside him on his right, sitting at the window end of the row of
back seats, had a covered basket on her lap. And as the quiet,
complaining conversational mew came again, she bent her
head close over the basket, opened the lid a crack, and murmured to the occupant: "Hush. Hush! We'll be home very
soon."

Looking up she met the eyes of Middlemass. He smiled at
her—she was a small, thin, dark girl, not unlike the one at the
desk in the gallery. And, like the girl in the gallery, she did not
return his smile, just gave him a steady, thoughtful look, as if
it would take much more than a smile to make her trust him,
or allow him to impinge on any of her concerns.

Rebuffed, he turned his head away and rose to his feet; the bus had reached his stop, anyway.

Returned home, he sat down at his desk, impatiently turning his back on the untidiness which, hurrying out into the sunny morning, he had promised himself that he would later set to rights.

He pulled an official college report form toward him, and, in the blank for Instructor's Name, printed MRS. MARCIA SCHABER. In the blank for Subject, he wrote LISTENING. In the blank for Observer, he wrote his own name, Prof. John Middlemass, and the date. Then, in the section headed "Comments" he began to write:

"Mrs. Schaber has something very important to teach her students, but I am not sure what it is. . . ."

There he stopped, holding the pen, staring at the blank form and his own name printed across the Observer space, while his mind's eye went back to fix, again, on the melancholy, huddled, crippled figure, gagged, blindfolded, beseeching, mutely extending his own name out of the wooden frame.

Sailors' Legends

Oh, that was a pretty place! The road corkscrewed down to it, so deep, so green between those high banks, and silent all the way but for a distant lark overhead like a watch ticking in the sky. Often there would be a mist with the sun peering through it and all the drops on the telegraph wires and thorn hedges shining brighter than angels' eyes.

It was the stillness, the green breathing dampness, the stretches of light reflected up to the sky from the wet road that stayed in your mind and the scent of primroses. I believe they had primroses all the year round, though they said not.

The first time I went I'd been washed up from a wreck: tossed like a bit of flotsam onto a black rock of those northern cliffs. I clambered up, blind and dazed from spray and battering, dragging my sea chest behind me. When I got to the top I looked back: miles and miles of hungry foam, snarling and curling; no sign of ship or shipmates save a spar or two floating in the dark blue. Later I learned they'd all been picked up by an Atlantic liner, but at the time I felt like the only man in the world.

I was strung out tight: next to playing my last note. I stumbled on, over the heather and gorse, toward Fernhoe. Only I didn't know it then. All of a sudden, the land began to fold in, the sky began to open out, and I was at the head of that lane, Sugarfoot Lane some of them called it, or Deepsea Lane.

Down I went. There wasn't a bird singing in the whole parish, only sometimes a curlew tuning up his sad scale. At every turn I expected houses, for there was a lived-in feel to the lane, purposeful. It was going somewhere as fast as it could. Sometimes a stream galloped by the road, sometimes great yews brooded guard on the bank or an avenue of silvery beeches kept me company along a stretch of the way. Then over a bit of hilltop and down I plunged into the steepest, deepest-arched hollow that ever carried a human foot.

This would be the place for snowdrops, I thought, and then I was around a corner and out in the village.

White houses, set about all anyhow, a bit of grass in the middle where the brook ran chuckling, fuchsias, palms, and cabbages all tangled up.

A boy was chopping logs on an open patch by the nearest house. I jerked down my box out of my stiffened arm and crossed over to him. He stood up, smiling, screwing his eyes against the bright sky. Eighteen or nineteen he would be, brown-haired and blue-eyed the way they come sometimes in the West Country, his head the shape and color of a glossy hazelnut.

"Can I get a bed in this village?" I asked.

"My mother, Widow Santo, sometimes puts up sailors," he said.

"I'm a sailor," I told him. "I've been washed ashore up back over. The ship went down last night—*Happy Alice*, from Bristol."

"It's a bad coast," he said, nodding. He lifted his axe and dropped it into a block of wood, shook the hair from his eyes, and said, "I'll take you to her."

She put you in mind of an orchard, the Widow Santo: fresh and peaceful and sweet smelling. She gave me a basin of soft cold water to wash in, and I flung myself out on a white coverlet and slept the day out and the dusk in.

"It's a quiet place, Fernhoe," she said at teatime. "Nobody talks much here. And in Coldharbor they never talk at all."

"Where's Coldharbor?"

"Up the valley." She pointed west. "Follow the road, follow the stream, and you'll come to it. Beyond Coldharbor you can't go. The moor closes in and the cliffs reach back. They don't get much disturbance up there. When folks think it's not peaceful enough here, they mostly go on up to Coldharbor."

Fernhoe certainly wasn't what you'd call a noisy place. You could hear a cock crow good morning or the clink of a spade on stone and that was about all. But Coldharbor was quieter still.

I walked up there when I'd rested two or three days. The village was smaller than Fernhoe and all set round a bridge over the stream, full here, smooth and noiseless. Old men leaned in the sunshine, roses in their buttonholes, smoking their pipes, and their wives sat shelling peas in doorways. They smiled as you went by but never spoke.

Past the village the hill ran up sharply to a cliff. Sometimes, standing there, you could feel rather than hear a distant boom and thump as the sea cast itself angrily against rocks beyond and to the north. A kind of hum and shiver ran through the village then, and there would be silence until the next time.

"The valley curves round, you see, like a horseshoe, us at one end and them at the other," Charley Santo said one evening as he sat putting a whipping on a bit of rope. "You're nearer to the sea in Coldharbor than you are here."

"You'd do well for a sailor," I told him, watching his skillful hands. "Ship along with me next time?"

"I'll never leave here." His smile was broad, and I knew he wouldn't budge; one might as well try to get a bird to leave its nest and live in one's pocket.

"Well, I must be off," I said to Mary Santo one day. "Time I was finding another ship. I shall miss you and Charley though. I've been right happy here."

"You'll come back," she said. "People mostly do."

She was right, I felt.

"Can I leave my chest here?" I asked. "There's nothing in it but old rubbish. It's not worth the carrying."

She hesitated. I had a sort of hope she'd say yes. Wandering as I knew myself to be, I thought that chest would pull me back. But finally she shook her head.

"It might bring bad luck," she said. "Things left unused go stale and turn to poison. You'd best take it with you."

And so she waved me off, with Charley beside her.

I shipped on a china-clay boat at St. Maul, and soon after my luck began to turn. I had one bit of fortune and then another: a good win, a windfall from an old aunt, a share in a piece of salvage, and in no time I was buying my own old tramp from a master who'd taken to drink and let her go downhill. *Katharina*, she was called, a Norwegian boat.

Only one of the crew came with her, a boy who'd just signed on. His name was Lars, and he came from some skerry in the far north where the sun shines at midnight and they have moss instead of grass. Lars was about seven feet tall, long and lanky, with a mop of lint-colored hair and a strawberry-burnt nose.

"Hey!" I said the first day, when he nearly dropped a tar-drum on my head. "How long have you been at sea?"

With a grin he told me he'd just left college; this was his first trip.

"But I'll soon learn," he said. He did too. He was quick and handy: a good boy.

He had a fiddle with him, and in between times he'd sit on the coaming and fetch tunes from it that shook your heart into a dance or made the blood run cold and slow in your veins from grief; it seemed queer to me sometimes that he had all that joy and amazement and despair locked up in him and yet didn't know it; when he put the violin down he was just seven feet of lanky boy. He used to fool about with the men and called me Paparuto, out of some book he'd been reading. From another boy I wouldn't have taken it, but he meant it in fun, no disrespect. He was a good boy.

One evening—it was off Gibraltar, warm and still—I remember a whole navy of swallows had settled in the rigging and were keening and whistling; he'd been playing his fiddle, and when he'd put it by and the men who had been clustered to listen had drifted away, I suddenly thought to tell him about Fernhoe and Coldharbor and the widow and Charley Santo.

It seemed odd to think of larks and primroses in this warm Mediterranean dusk with the gaggle of shipping round us, guttural shouts and accordion music coming from the Italian coaster alongside.

Lars was keen to hear all I could tell him. "It sounds like a place I read about once in a book," he said. A great one for reading, he was.

"I'd like you to meet Charley Santo," I said. Somehow I felt the two boys ought to know one another, almost that they belonged together. But Charley had a peacefulness in him that was lacking from Lars, who was restless and teasing as a fox cub; it seemed to me that Charley could teach Lars something important.

Oddly, although Lars liked to hear about the village and several times asked me to describe it again, he always turned sulky if I said too much about Charley. It seemed to bring uppermost a childish, unhappy side of his nature. Finally, I decided this was because of his boyhood. His mother had run away soon after he was born, and her name was never spoken. His father, a pastor, was a harsh, silent man, turned in on himself. In that solitary place the boy had been his own company or had found it from books and his fiddle. Until he went to college, he'd never met boys of his own age.

"Did you never see your mother again?" I asked him once.

"She died. . . . No, I never saw her. I found a picture of her once."

He showed it to me, much rubbed and with a furry sheen from traveling in his wallet—you couldn't distinguish much beyond a fair-haired, laughing face resting on interlinked fingers the way they used to take pictures. She had a look of Lars though; you could see that. I would have been curious to meet her—this mother who could run off and leave her boy.

Of course I wanted to take him to Mary Santo.

Well, we roamed about the saltwater world and, it may have been the next Christmas after that—Christmas time it was at all events—we fetched up at Plymouth. You'll hardly believe it, but I was excited as a boy at the thought of seeing my friends at Fernhoe and taking them presents. Naturally I wanted Lars to come along with me and be introduced.

At first he seemed willing enough, but we had to spend two or three days in Plymouth while I was busy with refitting, and during that time he took up with a girl. To hear him speak you'd think she was the eighth wonder of the world, but I had plenty of friends in Plymouth, and before long I heard a tale or two about her that made me worry. Melina Yeo, her name was, half Greek, half Devon, a slippery mixture. The boy was mad about her, and when, on the afternoon of Christmas Eve, my jobs done, I invited him to come over to Fernhoe with me, he fell into a silent sulk. Melina wanted him to take her out that evening, it seemed, though he'd taken her out every evening past and spent every penny of his money on her.

In the end I made him come, almost by force.

The coach didn't go all the way. We had to take it to a crossroads on the moor, then get out and walk. I'd have liked to get away earlier but was held up, waiting for a delivery of stores, and early winter dusk was falling when we started.

You can guess what happened. Before we'd walked a couple of miles of the ten that lay between us and Fernhoe, it was black dark and snow was beginning to fall. After an hour or so I had to confess I must have missed my landmarks and was properly lost.

We were lucky to find a barn with some hay in it, high up on the moor, where we had to resign ourselves to spending Christmas Eve.

Lars was in a black temper. I'd never known him quite like it before. Usually he came out of his sulks quick enough.

"To think I could have been with Melina," he muttered to himself as we made the best of the scanty hay, more than half marsh reed and thistle.

"You be thankful you're not, my lad," I said, provoked by my own failure to find the way. "She'd be picking your bones by this time. Where I'm taking you the people help sailors; they don't rob them."

"Where you're taking me!" he cried angrily. "Where you're taking me doesn't exist! Haven't you realized that yet? It's a dream village; it's not on any map. Of course you haven't found it, and you never will! I know all about it. It's in Homer and the Norse sagas and the Red Indian legends—"

"Do you mean to tell me that you've sat there listening to me talk about the place and you haven't believed me—?"

"Of course I haven't believed you," he said. "Oh, I know *you* believe it—but you were sleepwalking, or shocked; it was all a hallucination! This Fernhoe of yours is no more than a sailor's myth!"

"I'll show you in the morning that it isn't," I said, and I curled myself up in the parsimonious hay. But I was troubled, deep into my sleep, by the harsh unhappy certainty in his words. Could he possibly be right? Could it all have been a dream?

When I woke after my cold stiff slumber in the dusk of the morning, I found that I was not going to be able to prove anything to Lars, even if I could find Fernhoe, for he had gone.

He must have waited till I was asleep. A line of his footprints in the snow led back in the direction of Plymouth.

I went the other way. But once you are lost on those moors you are thoroughly lost, and though I searched the whole of Christmas day, I never found my landmarks and at last had to turn back, thumb a lift along the main road, and abandon the thought of seeing my friends.

And all the time under this unhappiness the thought of Lars was like an extra knot of bewildered pain.

By the time I reached the ship, the men were all assembled: we were due to sail at midnight. The only one not there was Lars; he turned up very late, without his duffel coat and fiddle, and avoided meeting my eye.

It was a short, sad trip. Somehow I found—and I think he felt the same—that I could not bear to talk to Lars. He jumped ship at Marseilles, and I made no push to get him back. One of the men told me later that he'd sold his fiddle to buy something for the girl and that then, having milked him dry, she'd walked off quite coolly and left him for someone else.

For months afterwards I felt as if I'd lost a son. Worse, the memory of Fernhoe was somehow twisted and saddened; I wasn't sure that even if I could find it, I could bear to go back. Deliberately I kept to other waters and steered clear of the Bristol Channel and Plymouth Sound.

Time went by. I wasn't getting any younger, and, what was worse, I was becoming seized up with arthritis and knew that one of these days I must make my last trip, say good-bye to the old *Katharina*, and step ashore for good. And who then would take me in, where would I settle?

It was at some devilish little port in the Mediterranean—I stayed where it was warm these days—that the British Consul asked me if I would take on a distressed seaman—not a British citizen, but his mother had been British and he was ill and the Consul was sorry for him.

You have guessed who it was, of course.

I was shocked when I saw him. He had aged twenty years, he was gaunt, his bones stood out like the ribs of a wreck, his face was a haggard shell with a mat of beard. But his eyes were as blue as ever.

"What have you been doing with yourself?" I said.

"Seeing the world," he said and coughed. "Collecting sailors' legends." He gave me a hint of grin. I wanted to get his poor wasted carcass bedded down in a bunk, but he wouldn't hear of it, said he would work his passage to wherever we were going. By chance I'd just been offered, and had just accepted, a consignment of tobacco for Bristol, knowing as I did so that by returning to a home port I was acknowledging this to be my last voyage.

Lars said Bristol would do well enough for him; he could pick up a Norwegian ship and make his way home. He was going back, he said, to try and find some of his father's family. Myself, I doubted if he would last the trip out; whenever he coughed, it seemed as if he would shake all his ribs apart.

Up in the Bristol channel we struck a November gale; I've met dirtier weather many a time, but I was anxious to get the ship back to port in good fettle and grieving because this was my last trip, besides being sick at heart about Lars. Wearing the ship through the midnight storm was almost more than I could tackle. Lars surprised me. He'd plainly learned a thing or two on his trips about the world, and in spite of his cough he was as good in the storm as two men.

And then, stupidly, when the blow was almost over and the seas were dying down, I had to go and fall overboard like a green boy—tired out, I was, and stiff, and so I just let a slanting wave knock my feet from under me.

None of the men saw me go. It was dark, and they were all over on the other side, battening down a bit of deck cargo that threatened to break loose. I knew that with my stiffened joints I could never swim. Drowning's as good a death as any, I supposed . . . and then Lars was beside me, his beard washed to a point and his eyes gleaming in the dark.

"On your back," he said. "Take it easy, I've got you." His arm swung me over.

"Crazy boy—" I gasped. "Why didn't you tell one of the men—?"

"No time. Keep your breath for swimming."

I searched the dark in vain for the lights of a boat. The *Katharina* seemed to have disappeared completely. Very probably no one had yet noticed we were missing, and when they did, what faintest chance was there that they would find us?

"You shouldn't have done it, Lars."

"Save your breath for swimming," he said again. I could hear his, in his chest, rasping like a faulty pump. But still he managed to keep us moving through the water. I couldn't do much to help; my legs felt numb and stiff, no longer part of me.

Presently we began to hear breakers, and—unbelievably, miraculously—out of the cold winter dawn I saw for a second time those black cliffs that I had climbed so many years before.

"Fernhoe," I gasped. "Up those cliffs. Fernhoe and Coldharbor." I felt my arm scrape on a rock, and the combined force of a wave and of Lars pushing hoisted me on to it. I gripped a ledge and reached down to haul him up, but the same wave, retreating, tugged him back.

"I'm done, Paparuto," he whispered. "Can't make it." And he sank like a stone.

So here I am, sitting on the spray-washed rocks, waiting for the sun to rise. Shall I, with my numb, stiff, old man's joints, be able to climb the cliff that was almost too much for me fifteen years ago? Or will the rising tide wash me off the rocks like a bundle of soaked straw?

Whatever happens, I'm not worrying about it very much. I've been thinking about Lars. Somehow I believe that I shall see him again and that it will be soon. And whether it is in Fernhoe, where they hardly speak, or in Coldharbor, where they never speak at all, what does it matter?

A Game of
Black and White

Toby Gage woke up with mixed feelings of happiness and
dread. Why? He rolled over in bed and then remembered. Today was his birthday. Good—very good. His father was going
to take him to a movie after school—which was a great conces-
sion, for his father didn't think much of films and hardly ever
went to one. But this was *Space Saga*, supposed to be very gripping. His mother was coming too, of course, if she felt well
enough; she didn't always, these days.

The birthday, therefore, was the happiness—but the dread?
Then he remembered. Old Saracen's history lesson. Mr. Sarson, his real name was; everyone called him Old Saracen. He
had an extraordinary habit, when he knew it was somebody's
birthday—he would call that boy out in front of the whole
class and publicly, violently, pull his hair. What a weird thing
to do. Why did he do it? Nobody knew. Nobody had dared
complain. He called it a passing-out ritual. It wasn't so much
having his hair pulled that horrified Toby—that had happened
to him often enough—it was the thought of having it done like
that in front of the whole class. Enough to make you die of
shame.

Then, having remembered so far, he also remembered that
it was all right: he had no need to worry. He had cunningly
suggested to his mother that, since a bit had broken off one of
his teeth, he needed to go to the dentist. (The bit had broken
off weeks ago, in fact, but she didn't know that. Toby had told

her it was urgent, that every time he chewed on something, he nearly hit the ceiling.) "Very well, darling, you make an appointment to see Dr. Ashburn," she had said, and Toby, phoning the dentist, had been lucky enough to get an appointment at twelve noon on his birthday morning—the very hour when he should have been doing history with Mr. Sarson and having his hair pulled.

No doubt Old Saracen would be hopping mad—"Why couldn't you get it done *after* school, Gage, may I ask?"— "Well, sir, I was in such pain—"

He would get his mother to write a note about it. Everything was okay.

Greatly relieved, he bounced out of bed, then remembered that something else exciting was going to happen today. The eclipse of the sun. Fancy having that happen on your birthday. What a thing!

"You're an Eclipse child!" his mother said, teasing him, at breakfast.

Breakfast was a hasty meal, as usual. Toby had to get off to school, and his father, who ran a large plant nursery just outside the town of Solchester, where they lived, was fussed because of a request he'd had from a bulb grower in Lincolnshire —"Wants me to accommodate a whole field of tulips for him, bit of a nuisance, just now." "A whole *field*, darling, what *do* you mean?" "Oh, bulb growers do that sometimes, ask other gardeners to have their bulbs for a year, if they haven't got the space or think the bulbs need a different kind of soil—I've kept this chap's bulbs for him before now. But this time it really is a bit much—he's sending the bulbs down *today*— a whole field of black tulips—they'll have to be planted right off—it'll need at least three men and a tractor, which I can't spare—"

Annoyed, preoccupied, Mr. Gage got up to leave. He hadn't forgotten his son's birthday, though. By Toby's plate was a beautiful birthday card of two zebras fighting and a large, flat, square package. Toby guessed immediately what it was: a record.

"And I bet I know what it is, Dad."

"Handel wrote those tunes when he was ten," Mr. Gage said, his face clearing, the worried, busy frown leaving it for a moment. He ruffled Toby's hair. "There's still time for *you* to get busy, wonder boy!" Toby wrote tunes too. He took the wrapping paper off the record and saw that it was six trio sonatas for two Oboen, Faggot und Cembalo, Handel's Opus No. 1.

"Opus One means the first piece of music he ever wrote," Mr. Gage said.

"I don't suppose that's really true. I read somewhere he was writing tunes at six," Toby said. "I expect it's the earliest they've managed to find."

"Well, I have to dash," his father said, "if all those tulips are going to be planted this afternoon. See you then. Don't take any wooden pennies." Mr. Gage always said that; *his* father— Grandfather—had said it to him.

Toby had a card (roses) from his mother, but no present yet: his present from her was going to be a bicycle, and he was going to meet her at a quarter to one, after the dentist, in Ptolemy's, the only big department store in the town, where they had a good sports department, in order to choose one. Toby was vaguely aware that his mother had money of her own, that in a way she was quite rich, whereas his father only had what came in from the nursery. So her presents were often bigger and grander. It made no difference: he liked his father's presents just as much.

"See you at Tolly's, then, Mom." Toby prepared to rush off in his turn.

"Don't forget the dentist, will you, darling. I *do* hope he doesn't hurt you too much," Mrs. Gage said anxiously. That was the sort of thing that did make her anxious—she was a gentle person, easily scared.

"I'll be okay—honest," Toby told her, feeling a fraud.

He raced off to school—the old Grammar School, now Intermediate, right in the center of town, with a big chestnut tree growing in front. Some of the buildings were three hundred years old. There were more buildings now—more modern ones—on the edge of town, but Toby thought he was lucky—only five minutes' run from home to school.

The first lesson of the day was geography, and Mr. Marsh explained about eclipses and drew diagrams of suns and moons on the blackboard, and told them about eclipse tracks, nodes, apexes, partial eclipses and annular eclipses—rather more than they really wanted to know.

Then it was gym, then break, then English, then Toby had to go to the dentist; he laid his mother's note on the desk, ready for Old Saracen, and dashed away without waiting for the explosion.

He was lucky in his dentist's location, too. Dr. Ashburn had his office in North Street, only three minutes from the Butter Cross in the middle of town where the four streets met. Down one street and up another. . . . Four minutes' dash.

"Go right in," said the white-coated receptionist. "He's waiting for you."

The office had a window looking into a small disused graveyard. Toby went in and settled himself in the dentist's chair without being told. Dr. Ashburn had installed the very last word in modern equipment: he had a high-speed drill, and his dentist's chair dangled on a kind of pulley. Patients lay flat on their backs and gazed at the ceiling (which was all painted over with the sun, moon, and stars) while the dentist, in another chair, spun round on a track, peering at cavities.

"Just like the solar system, really," Dr. Ashburn remarked. "You're probably free from gravity, too, hanging from the ceiling like that." He was joking, but Toby said, "Haven't they got something dangling from the dome of St. Paul's that's gradually working its way round in a circle, so as to prove that the world goes round?"

"Really? Haven't they proved that yet? Now, open wide, please."

Dr. Ashburn did a bit of work in Toby's mouth, then

rubbed his forehead and said, "Look, I'm terribly sorry, Toby, but I've got a shocking headache all of a sudden. Eclipse weather—I daresay that's what's giving it to me. Would you mind if we leave it for now—I've put you in a temporary filling?"

"Of course not," said Toby. After all, that meant he'd have some free time off from school. He could go and give the bikes in Ptolemy's a really careful once-over before his mother got there. He said, "I'm awfully sorry your head's bad, Dr. Ashburn."

"I'll take something for it and lie down on the sofa for a couple of hours. You could come back after afternoon school if you like—about four? I've done all the drilling—the nasty part's over—there's only a bit more filling to do."

"All right," said Toby. "Might as well get it over. I come out of school at four—I could be here by five past."

He ran out joyfully into the hot sun—then remembered that quite soon now it would be gone. How queer! Better go and do his choosing at Tolly's before the eclipse began—he wanted to see that. He ran down North Street, along West Street, into Ptolemy's. Up the escalator to the second floor, where the sports department was. Twenty minutes to look at bikes before his mother got there.

Slowly and carefully he studied all the makes there—Ptolemy's had a really good selection, there were plenty to choose from—when suddenly he heard a voice—"*There* you are, darling, already. You must have got here early."

Startled, he turned around, and, after a second, said very embarrassed, "I—I think—aren't you making a mistake?"

For the woman who had greeted him was not his mother. Curiously enough, though, she did look very like Mrs. Gage—a tallish, thinnish, dark woman, wearing rather smart dark clothes. What was *really* odd was that she had a bird sitting on her shoulder—a small, skinny white bird with a white crest; the bird was attached to her wrist by a very fine chain.

The woman ignored Toby's stammered remark and said, smiling, "Well—? Have you chosen a bike yet, Toby?"

Beginning to think she must be some friend of his mother's who had arranged to meet them here (What a bore! On his birthday?), Toby said. "Well, I had been thinking of this one—"

"Splendid. That looks like a very good choice. My son will have this one," the woman instantly said to a sales clerk hopefully hovering near; he had been keeping an eye on Toby for the last ten minutes, as if expecting him to mount one of the bikes and ride off with it.

"But wait! I don't understand! *You're* not my mother," expostulated Toby, very much upset, and he said to the assistant, "I'm not her son!" The man looked baffled, then smiled sympathetically at the dark woman. Now, with great relief, Toby saw his own mother at the far end of the large department, beyond all the bicycles, and he called out joyfully, "There she is! There's my mother!"

"Don't be silly," the dark woman said coldly. "Stop playing the fool, please, Toby. She has her own boy with her—you can see that."

And indeed Mrs. Gage was being greeted by a boy in school clothes who did have a kind of resemblance to Toby himself. Toby felt more and more bewildered and horrified. Am I mad? he thought. Or is she?

"Mother! *mother!*" he called, but Mrs. Gage, talking to the other boy, never looked his way.

"Come on now, come on, let's get this bike bought," exclaimed the dark woman, irritably. "I know it's your birthday —but that's no excuse for idiotic behavior. This one, you said you wanted?"

The sales clerk, who was evidently concealing intense interest under his weary manner, suddenly perked up and got out his receipt book.

"Cash or charge, Madam?" he asked briskly.

Toby, wretched, puzzled, still trying to attract his own

mother's attention, had no interest in whether the bike was bought or not. But he was suddenly startled by a piercing whisper in his ear.

"Don't let her buy anything for you!"

He looked around in astonishment. Who had spoken? He could see no one, except the dark woman and the man writing in his book.

The whisper came again. "Don't let her buy you a bicycle!"

Then Toby realized that it was the bird that had spoken— the thin white bird chained to the woman's wrist. "Don't take anything from her!" it hissed.

"I don't want a bike, thanks!" Toby said loudly and rudely. The man stopped writing, startled. "Don't write any more," Toby said again. "I don't want it."

"Dear me, how very changeable," the woman said with a cold laugh. She was obviously very annoyed. "Well, if you don't want a bike. I suppose there's no point in our staying here. We might as well go home. Perhaps you'll presently think of something else that you *do* want?"

Grasping Toby's wrist with surprising strength, she steered him toward the escalator, without apologizing to the clerk for all his needless trouble. Toby looked wretchedly back toward his real mother—but she appeared not to have seen him; she was deep in conversation with that other boy. Perhaps she was not his mother at all? Who *am* I? Toby wondered. If I'm not her son, do I have to go with this woman? He did not want to in the least—he felt a strong, instinctive dislike for her. But what else could he do? Where could he go?

At the foot of the escalator they found themselves in the carpet department. Huge unrolled rugs lay all over the floor; others, rolled up, leaned like ghosts against the walls. It was a spooky place and made more so by the darkness that filled it now. All around Toby could hear chatter, laughter, girls letting out squeaks of fright. It was the beginning of the eclipse. He had forgotten all about it.

"Come on!" the woman said sharply. She dragged Toby to-

ward a side entrance—a small door half hidden between two
rolls of carpet. He had never noticed it before. Once through
it, they found themselves, unexpectedly enough, in a small
enclosed graveyard. Not so surprising really—the town was
full of such odd little enclosures, ancient plots and gardens in
among the old houses.

A strange lurid light filled the deserted little place, where
the gravestones were tilted at all sorts of odd angles. It became
darker and darker; the sky overhead turned from yellow to
gray to black. Stars shone out, and the tombstones began to
shine with a dim, phosphorescent light of their own.

How strange, Toby thought, looking around. They are all
chess pieces. I never heard of tombstones being shaped like
chess pieces before.

Queens, bishops, knights were leaning toward each other—
they looked as if they were signaling, talking to each other.
Glancing around to see what had become of the dark woman,
Toby saw that she, too, wore a crown, a black crown.

"Stand there!" she ordered Toby, pointing. "You are nothing but a pawn; that is *your* place."

Moving mechanically among the gravestones, Toby noticed,
at one side, a square tomb of the enclosed kind: a stone box,
big as a grand piano. One of its walls, though, was transparent
crystal, and inside it sat a woman—his mother, surely?—all
dressed in white robes, with her head bent forward.

"Mother, mother!" he screamed.

"She can't hear you," said the Black Queen. "Go to your
place."

The woman in the tomb had her head bowed in grief over a
baby she was holding; it was all wrapped in swaddlings. She
did not hear Toby.

Despairing, he looked around and saw a light at the end of
the graveyard: a window in a house there. Then—of course—
he realized where he was. It was the graveyard outside Dr.
Ashburn's window—he was actually looking right into the office. There was a chair, the gleaming instruments, the drill,

the porcelain basin. A huge feeling of relief rushed into Toby's heart. These things at least were real, were sensible and practical!

With an almost intolerable effort—he felt as if his shoes were weighted with iron, were being pulled to the ground by magnets—he ran slowly to the window and tapped on it. Dr. Ashburn was lying on a sofa at the back of the office. After what seemed to Toby a long and terrifying time, he came to the window and pushed up the sash.

"Why, Toby! Do you want to come in?"

"Oh, *yes!*" said Toby and climbed over the sill. With inexpressible relief, he heard Dr. Ashburn close the sash behind him.

"How is your headache, Dr. Ashburn?" he remembered to ask.

"It is getting better slowly. What has been happening to you, Toby?"

"May I get into your dentist's chair, Dr. Ashburn?"

"Certainly, if you want to."

Toby climbed into the chair, lay back in it, and swung himself around a couple of times. Then he told Dr. Ashburn what had happened. The dentist did not seem surprised.

"Light and dark," he said. "They are polarized at the time of eclipse.

"The dark is always there, of course, mixed in; but at some periods it has more power than others. And you being born today—you say you were born at twelve noon?"

"Yes," said Toby.

"Then you are specially vulnerable."

"But what can I do?" said Toby. "How can I get back my real mother? How can I get rid of that—that woman?"

Dr. Ashburn pressed his fingers against his forehead as if the pain might burst out at any minute. He said, "You had better run barefoot around the town wall. If you can do that while the eclipse is still going on—"

"Then I'd better start at once!" exclaimed Toby. "How long does it last?"

"Not long. Yes, you'd better hurry. When you've been all the way around—back to the graveyard."

"The graveyard?" said Toby, not liking that.

"There you have a choice. You see those angels on the tomb —one with a trumpet, the other playing a drum—?" Toby did see them, through the window; the chess pieces were no longer visible.

"You have to blow on the trumpet or beat on the drum. I am not sure which. *You* will have to decide. Now—*run!*"

Toby flung off his shoes, which he left in the waiting room, and ran out barefoot into the street. It was dark, with a strange yellowish black sky overhead, in which pale stars dimly shone. The birds were letting out terribly anxious cries. Dogs were whining. There were no streetlights on, since they worked by time clock; consequently, all traffic had come to a stop. People were talking, laughing, and exclaiming in the gloom. Toby fled past them as if they were ghosts and ran to the top of North Street, up the winding steps that led to the top of the town wall. It was the old rampart, the old Roman wall; there was a track all the way around the top. Which way should he go, clockwise or counterclockwise? He decided on clockwise and started off, running as fast as he could go, gulping in the suddenly cold air. He could feel it in his chest; it seemed to be taking up more and more room, a great ball of freezing air. He wondered how long he could bear it. The gravel path hurt his feet; several times he stubbed his toes. On and on he ran. Sometimes he passed people looking at the sky through telescopes; at one point he saw Old Saracen the history master, who made a grab at his hair, and shouted, "Why weren't you in class, you naughty wretch?" "I'm not afraid of *you!*" shouted Toby, and raced on.

Turning at the southeast corner of the town, he could see his father's nursery-garden greenhouses gleaming dimly in the distance, and he found time to wonder how they were getting on with planting the tulips—a whole field of black tulips! Very difficult in the dark, he thought, and then gasped as he turned another corner and came face to face with the sun. But what a sun! Black, red-black in the middle, but all around it, flaming out for hundreds of miles into space, huge red leaping fiery shapes, like snakes, like monsters, like crocodiles, the dragons —Toby dared take only a brief glance; he must keep his eyes on the narrow track. On, on, he ran, past the cathedral tower, past the Granada theater, past the gasworks and the train station, the bus station, and Tothams' factory, over the river and the canal. Now he turned another corner and this was his last. Down the steps—along North Street, sobbing for breath— into West Street and through the little rusty gate into the graveyard. Gulping with relief—for the sky was still dark, he had done it in time—he ran to the big stone tomb.

Now, which? The trumpet or the drum? He had no breath left for blowing. It must be the drum. Snatching the stone drumstick from the angel's grasp, he beat a loud tattoo on the carved drum. But his drumming was drowned in a tremendous sound of car horns, factory sirens, gongs beating, and people shouting outside in the street. A bright red light was beginning to show in the sky: the sun was coming out of its eclipse.

But under all the row, Toby thought that he could hear a sound of infinitely sad weeping; he was horrified to see, in the crystal tomb, the white-robed woman bow her head over the motionless child and wring her hands together in despair. . . .

Toby climbed back through Dr. Ashburn's window.

"Did I make the wrong choice?" he demanded. "Should it have been the trumpet, after all?"

"I'm afraid so," Dr. Ashburn said sadly. "Not your fault. How could you tell? You'll choose again another time—many, many more times—sometimes you'll get it right. Now," the dentist added in a brisk manner, "as my headache has gone, we had better get that filling dealt with. Do you want to put your shoes on first?"

When the filling was done, Toby ran home fast. He found his father there, unexpectedly early.

"I'm afraid your mother has been taken ill," he explained.

"*Badly?*" Toby was terrified.

"No, she'll be all right. But she lost the child—she's very sad about that." Toby knew that his mother had been going to have another baby. "So I'm afraid we won't be able to go out and leave her alone tonight. You won't mind, will you?"

"Of *course* not," Toby said. "Shall I go—shall I go up and see her?"

"Yes, do, she'd like that."

Toby went up to his mother's room, where she lay propped on pillows. He hugged her in silence. "Never mind, Mom," he said presently. "Never mind." She was crying a little; he gave a great sniff himself. After a while he said, "You'll be able to have another one, won't you? By and by?"

She nodded, faintly smiling.

"That's good," Toby said. "I'll bring you up some tea, shall I?"

"That would be lovely, thank you, darling."

While he was putting the tea on a tray, Toby said to his father, "Did you get the tulips planted—the black tulips?"

Mr. Gage gave a snort. "Yes, we did—they worked like beavers all morning, got them in, and what do you think happened? This afternoon, just after the eclipse, while all the bulbs were still uncovered, ready to be earthed up, that fool Maddingley's crop-spray plane came over, and the pilot thought it was Maddingley's field; he sprayed the whole lot with Double X-Cop weedkiller—every one was ruined. Covered by insurance, of course, thank heaven—"

Toby took the tray up to his mother.

"I'm sorry I couldn't get to Ptolemy's, darling," she said weakly, sipping her tea. "I did phone though, but I don't suppose anyone remembered to give you the message—I was taken ill about then. I do hope you didn't wait long."

"Not long," said Toby.

"We'll get a bicycle another day. When I'm better."

"I think maybe I'd rather earn one," said Toby. "I'll start a paper route."

"All right, darling. If you'd rather."

"Shall I put on some music, Mom? Would you like that?"

"That would be lovely, darling."

So Toby put the record that his father had given him on the player and turned the volume up loud.

Beautiful music began to fill the house.

Elephant's Ear

"The fleas," said Miss Printer, "are not so bad here as they were at Sreb."

"Maybe not," said Mr. Humphreys, "but they are a lot worse than they were at Prijepolje. Have you finished buying wine?"

"I have plenty of slivovitz and riesling. But I'd like a few dozen more proseks and some retsina if we go home through Greece. How are you getting on?"

"I've bought a lot of hors d'oeuvres and twenty tapestries."

"We could do with some silver jewelery."

"We shall never be home by Christmas at this rate," grumbled Mr. Humphreys, a thin, dark, and irascible young man.

Miss Printer raised her fine brows and gazed at him reproachfully with enormous gray eyes, clear as November lochs. They were her best feature. She had passed her first youth, though she was still in her second; indeed there was a quality about the famous London store of Rampadges which seemed to preserve its employees, flavor and body, like the best ginger. Miss Printer had been with the firm no more than twenty years, since she was seventeen, but already, thin, smooth-skinned, pale-haired, she was touched with agelessness.

"Haven't you any loyalty to the firm?" she suggested.

When they set sail together on their buying excursion, she had been on the verge of falling in love with Mr. Humphreys.

Now she was over the brink, helpless and hopeless, and finding it an uphill emotion in the face of their differences.

"Surely we've bought enough for the Christmas market?"

"Enough staples," she said, considering their list. "French plums, Swiss cuckoo clocks, Czech embroidery, German toys. Not enough novelties. I'd like go down to Galicnik and buy some stonework."

"*Stonework?*"

"People like it for ornamental gardens. And I do wish we could get hold of an elephant or a kangaroo."

Mr. Humphreys had exhausted his capacity for expressing surprise. He just gaped at her and said at length rather feebly. "Surely it's not very probable in the Balkans?"

"Not *very*, but it's possible," said Miss Printer. "I have done so before. There are many traveling menageries in these parts. And since we are limited to Europe, the Balkans are our best bet."

"Why do you want elephants and kangaroos?"

"In Mr. Tybalt's day they always had an elephant at Rampadges for Christmas," she said wistfully. "Or a camel or a zebra."

"He's dead now."

"I know." No need to say more. Mr. Tybalt had been the nephew of the original Rampadge who started the magnificent store, and his ideas had been as lavish and imperial as those of his Victorian forebear.

The two travelers got back into their car, having finished their frugal picnic of prsut, borak, ratluk lokum, and Cvicek drunk from plastic mugs—although she was a discerning and intrepid buyer, Miss Printer did not believe in wasting the firm's money—and continued on their way, Mr. Humphreys driving.

They were bound for a small Montenegrin town called Grksik, where Miss Printer hoped to buy some pairs of the famous local slippers embroidered with gold thread and heavily jeweled, which should sell like hot cakes at Christmas.

The bleak, wild Balkan scenery rose about them in tarnished autumnal colors. It made Mr. Humphreys shiver, but Miss Printer surveyed it affectionately.

"I had such a nice picnic here in 1947," she said. Her tone of comfortable reminiscence somehow annoyed Mr. Humphreys, and he trod incautiously on the accelerator. Their powerful hired car zipped around a sharp turn in the road and became disastrously entangled with the rear section of a procession which had been concealed from them by a spur of the mountain.

"Zalvaro!"

"Molim, molim?"

"Oh dear."

"Au secours!"

"Oimoi!"

Shouts, bellows, brays, and polyglot exclamations volleyed from the ramshackle cornice of men, animals, and rudimentary vehicles which had toppled backwards over the hood of their car.

"Oh dear," said Miss Printer again, "you seem to have bumped into a circus."

By now it was nearly dark.

Miss Printer knew that in some European countries the adjective *Balkan* is used to describe something uncouth, wild, savage.

Balkan, she thought to herself with satisfaction, gazing at the crazy torchlit mass that settled over and around the front portion of their sedate car. Goats formed a kind of fringe to it; there were bearded, tarbooshed men with staves, like Old Testament illustrations; two apes, apparently chained together; and a zebra, neat and dainty as a fairytale convict. The whole scene gave Miss Printer a deep and inexplicable pleasure.

Mr. Humphreys was standing commandingly in the midst of it all, trying to make some sense out of the business. Her heart ached with love at the sight of him. He was so tall and well-cut and impeccable; his head was such a good shape; the curl on the bowler that he wore even in the Balkans was exactly right. He looked what he was, a young English businessman who would make good.

The best of his kind in the world, thought Miss Printer sorrowfully. If he had been an article for sale in the market, she would have bought him unhesitatingly for Rampadges, whatever his price. But he belonged to Rampadges already, and whatever his price, he was not for her; she knew that she filled him with alarm and a vague resentment.

He came angrily back to the car. "I can't get what they are saying," he said. "Can you make it out?"

Miss Printer uncoiled her slender length from the other front seat. She had fluent French, German, Italian, Turkish, and a smattering of Greek, Russian, and Spanish, but none of these proved effective in the present case, so she fell back on the Serbo phrase book.

"Molim rezervirati jednu sobu sa dva kreveta i kupatilom, Please reserve one double room with a bathroom," hardly seemed to meet the situation, but she tried, "Dobro vece, Good evening. Ne razumem, I do not understand. Zao mi je, I am sorry," and followed it up with, "Mogu li imati racun, molim? Can I have the bill, please?"

This produced a hush. The chorus sorted themselves out, and the goats were dragged offstage. A small boy led the zebra away into the dark, while the monkeys were tidied back into a sort of wicker baby carriage.

"Racun," she repeated hopefully.

An enormous smiling man with moustaches like brackets shouldered his way into the flaring light and burst into a torrent of explanation which Mr. Humphreys listened to in bewildered noncomprehension.

Miss Printer attended, nodding. A boy squatting beside them held a flashlight, so that she looked like a small cream-colored witch interviewing an affable devil. At length the man bowed, bringing down his arms in a sweeping gesture of acceptance. Some money changed hands.

The procession disentangled itself with almost magical speed and whirled off into the darkness.

"Well! You settled that easily," said Mr. Humphreys with unwilling respect. "How much did you have to give him?"

"Oh, only about thirty pence." Miss Printer spoke absently. She was straining her eyes, searching for something in the engulfing dark. "There was a condition attached, you see. We have injured one of the men, and the condition was that we take him and his animal to the nearest monastery."

"Injured a man?" said Mr. Humphreys, aghast.

"He fainted from fright so far as I could gather."

"And they just went off like that and left him? Where is he?"

"Somewhere around. The ringmaster, or whatever he was, said this man, Iskandar, was a weakling. He seemed rather glad to be rid of him. Yes, there he is." Her eye had caught a gleam of white and she moved away. When Mr. Humphreys caught up with her, she was kneeling by the side of what at first appeared to be a bundle of rags.

"He's still in a faint," she said. "We'd better get him into the back of the car before he comes to."

"Most extraordinary," Mr. Humphreys muttered, helping her lift the little man, who was piteously thin and light, no more than skin and bone. "What language were you talking to the ringmaster?"

"Turkish. But I think he said this man was a Russian."

Iskandar came to as they put him in and uttered a loud groan. At the same moment Mr. Humphreys felt himself suddenly plucked backwards into the air as if a spaceship had lowered a grapnel and removed him, dangling, from the earth. He had not even time to yell, could not believe in his predicament, but the gasp he gave as he left all his breath behind was enough to attract Miss Printer's attention.

"Oh, good gracious," she said, "what a coincidence. Though I suppose one might have expected it in the circumstances."

"Expected *what?*"

"An elephant. Just the same it does seem like a miracle."

With a characteristically irrelevant flight she added, "Isn't there a ballet called *Miracle in the Balkans?*"

"In the *Gorbals,*" snapped Mr. Humphreys, who was something of an expert on ballet. "If you speak any elephant language, will you tell it to put me down?"

Miss Printer did not speak elephant language, but she rummaged among the remnants of the picnic for pieces of turkish delight and with these persuaded the elephant to relinquish Mr. Humphreys, who climbed, fuming and rubbing himself, into the car.

"It's a very nice *little* elephant," Miss Printer said acquisitively. "I believe it's a female. I wonder how we can get it to the monastery. Do you suppose Iskandar would sell it?"

The night air was cool and smelled of dew and rock, and the mountainside was totally silent. They might have been all alone on the southern slopes of Europe. The elephant evidently felt lonely, for it drew nearer to the car and let out a plaintive sound somewhere between a gurgle and a hoot. The sick man in the car stirred and muttered an unintelligible answer.

"What language is that?" said Mr. Humphreys uneasily.

"Russian. Where did I put that bottle of Cvicek?" She delved once more among the picnic debris and found the wine and a cup.

"Probably the worst thing for him if he's suffering from shock," Mr. Humphreys pointed out gloomily. However Iskandar came to sufficiently under the influence of the wine to direct them to the nearest monastery and also to assure them that Chloe, the elephant, would follow peaceably behind the car if she might be allowed to put her trunk in at the window and feel her master sitting inside.

They started off slowly, Miss Printer a little disappointed, as she had been hoping in her romantic heart for an elephant ride through the moonlit uplands.

The brothers at the monastery took in Iskandar and his elephant without demur, and, as it was now late, invited Miss

Printer and Mr. Humphreys to stay for the night, giving them each a tiny guest cell.

In the small hours Miss Printer was wakened by knocking.

"Who is it?" she called sleepily.

"The sick man is asking for you," one of the brothers whispered through the keyhole. She hastily flung on clothes and followed him to the infirmary, a long bare stone room facing east over the windswept hillside. Already the dawn was beginning to show wild and green, like streaks of toothpaste in the sky.

The little man Iskandar, washed and snug, a tiny kernel in a large nut, lay peacefully in a white bed, with the sharp lines of his face filed keener by the sharp light.

"I am dying," he said matter of factly to Miss Printer as soon as she reached him. "You have a good face, so to you I entrust my elephant because she is a good elephant. She is a clever elephant too. She is over seventy years old and has seen the Czar of Russia when there was a czar. She has been left me by my father, who was a Russian landowner. After the revolution she was all that remained of his wealth. She and I escaped from Russia together, and since then we have wandered many hundreds of miles."

He gasped between his words and one of the brothers offered a drink.

Miss Printer was crying a little.

"Don't be disturbed," said Iskandar with a touch of impatience. "I have been journeying to this place for many years. I am glad to get here. All I ask of you is that you take care of Chloe—take particular care of her ears, please—and that you arrange for her to see, once, my younger brother in London. She will carry my dying message to him. You can do this? I have his address here, on a bit of paper." He fumbled at his small bundle of possessions and handed her a grubby scrap on which was written, in beautiful Cyrillic characters, the name Joachim Boyanus and a London address.

"Oh yes, I can easily do that."

"Good," he said, and glanced through the window. A sheepish-looking lay brother had Chloe outside, and at a command from her master she threaded her black snakelike trunk through the window. Iskandar caressed it almost absently and then passed it over to Miss Printer for mutual recognition and inspection.

"Now you must go," he said in a businesslike tone. "I am about to die."

Drawing closer about him, the brothers began a deep-toned chant.

"Don't distress yourself, miss," said the kindly infirmarian, who spoke good German. "It is not your fault he dies. In his condition it is amazing that he lived so long."

"But I had said that I wanted an elephant," Miss Printer wept. "And then to be given one like *this*. . . ."

"But you must think of Iskandar too," the monk pointed out benignly. "How fortunate for him to meet a trustworthy English lady to carry out his last wish." Much to Miss Printer's surprise, he gave her a cup of tea.

She wandered out into the windy dawn to escape from the sound of chanting and to become acquainted with her new responsibility.

Mr. Humphreys was frankly appalled when he heard of the matter and more so when he discovered that he and Miss Printer would have to ride on Chloe if they were ever to reach a port.

Their car, apparently suffering from delayed effects of the collision, completely refused to start, and the nearest mechanic was fifty miles off. At length Humphreys gave in. After the monks had celebrated Iskandar's funeral with every Orthodox rite, they piled their luggage on Chloe and rolled away southwards over the mountains.

"How you expect to get past customs and quarantine I've no idea," Mr. Humphreys said sourly, but Miss Printer was perfectly serene.

"We shall manage somehow," she said. "Chloe will take care

of us." And indeed Chloe took care of them to such good effect that they crossed two frontiers without troubling the Customs, sailing past the posts like something impalpable between dusk and dawn while once, when they were ambushed by Albanian bandits as they picnicked, Chloe picked up her two riders and stowed them about her person like a boy scout tucking knife and matches into his pockets and drifted away down a rocky hillside before the astonished brigands had their sights set for this unexpected safety device. That time Mr. Humphreys' bowler got left behind. It did not sweeten his attitude to Chloe.

In Athens, Miss Printer sent two cables, one to Joachim Boyanus, the other to her immediate superior at Rampadges:

DOCKING HULL NOON 19TH ON KATINA PAXINOU HAVE ELEPHANT TAPESTRIES STONEWORK CUCKOO CLOCKS ETC.

It was not her fault that the Greek telegraphist, always a bit shaky on translating to the Roman alphabet, should have sent the cable as ELEGANT TAPESTRIES STONE CUCKOO CLOCK WORKS. Nor could she have been expected to know, off in the wilds, as she and Mr. Humphreys had been for the last two months, that Rampadges had been the subject of a vast takeover bid and was now under new ownership.

Nor could she have foretold that the new managing director, Mr. Appelbee, had decided to come down to the docks for a personal inspection of the rare goods brought back for the Christmas market by the firm's most discerning buyer.

Chloe and Miss Printer had suffered on the voyage. The Greek ship was a tiny one, and neither of them was a good sailor. Mr. Humphreys, chilly, correct, and unsympathetic, had visited them both impartially with basins of arrowroot.

Mr. Appelbee was in an irritable mood the day the ship docked. He was a small, dyspeptic man who looked as if he had been scrubbed all over with a fine brush and the very best soap. He had found much to criticize already in Rampadges and was now wishing he had stayed in bed. The morning was bleak, the dock filthy, Hull a bad and foggy dream. And then the cuckoo clocks had turned out, most disappointingly, not to be made of stone at all, and the tapestries not all that elegant.

It was the last straw when Miss Printer, pale and unhappy, made her appearance on the wharf followed by a small green-ish elephant.

"What do you call *that?*" he snarled. "Have you been spending the firm's money on *that?* Well, I tell you frankly, you had better take the next boat back to where you've come from and get rid of it. There's no place for elephants in the new Rampadges—nor for damn fools who buy such damn-fool objects!"

Miss Printer looked round for Mr. Humphreys to give her moral support, but he had gone, walking elegantly off to chat to the manager of the Transport Department, and when she saw this craven betrayal the last shred of her love blew away in the chilly breeze.

She nerved herself.

"Mr. Appelbee," she said, "you may have got enough money to buy Rampadges, but you can't buy the loyalty of its employees. Loyalty has to be earned.

"I had intended to *give* Chloe to the firm, but I've changed my mind. Since she saved my life we've grown very close. Looking after her, taking the splinters out of her feet and washing her ears, has taught me something. You can give affection to an elephant that you can't give to a firm. Mr. Appelbee, I'm going to keep Chloe for myself, and here is my resignation for you. I'm sure you will find Mr. Humphreys an excellent buyer when he has learned a few more languages."

And she turned away, taking Chloe's trunk under her arm, and walked briskly along the dock. A dark and bearded man in a city suit came up to her.

"Miss Printer?" he said. "I am Joachim Boyanus. I thank you for letting me meet Chloe once again."

Chloe was delighted to see him. She wreathed her trunk round his neck.

"I have taken good care of her," said Miss Printer, looking at him very directly with her clear gray eyes. Joachim turned back the flap of one huge leather ear and saw a great many pieces of slate-colored sticking-plaster. Thoughtfully he pulled one loose and found under it a diamond as large as a hazelnut.

"Ah yes," he said. "The family diamonds. I wondered where Iskandar had hidden them all these years. It was kind of him to send them and kind of you to bring them. But really, you know, I have done so comfortably in the City that I hardly need them. Would you accept them, Miss Printer?"

"I?" She was dumbfounded.

"You have just left your job," he pointed out. "Could you not use them? What is your dearest wish?"

"Oh," she said, starry-eyed, "to travel, of course. To travel with Chloe."

"Miss Printer," he said, "you are a woman after my own heart. For some time I have been intending to leave the City, whose moneymaking possibilities I have explored to the uttermost, and wander off to an older and more peaceable world. Could we not go together, you and I and Chloe?"

They looked at one another, liking what they saw.

And since nothing is very difficult if two people are mutually attracted, and have plenty of money and a well-disposed elephant, it is probable that they are traveling still.

The Sewanee Glide

Old Miss Norah Murphy was slowly brushing out her thin, lank white hair, standing at the window, staring out into the untidy park where half the trees were dying. It was a brilliant autumn day: mist was rising fast off the silvered grass. Far away, beyond the trees, the pale, moonlike shapes of the Burren hills gleamed, like peeled hardboiled eggs, Miss Norah thought, continuing to brush, and she began slowly planning how she would have a hardboiled egg for her lunch, or maybe two. She knew in advance that her sister Maud would grumble and raise objections: "Worst thing in the world for your digestion. An apple and a raw carrot would be better for you—and a walnut or two." Maud was a vegetarian: she would eat nothing that had come from any animal. It was really just an outlet for her natural bossiness, her younger sister decided.

One of the trees that were still in good health, a great handsome walnut, was slowly turning from dull green to pale yellow; here and there a lemon-colored frond fluttered down. And the nuts in their bruised green cases were thudding to the ground like golf balls. We ought to go out this day and collect them, Miss Norah thought, or the squirrels will get the lot of them. Maud won't want to. You'd think she'd see the necessity, and she so fond of a walnut. I don't know at all what's got into her these days. You'd think it was a walled-in convent, the way she sits inside the livelong day and carries on like the Emperor Tiberius if I so much as set foot out of doors.

A couple of squirrels were out under the tree, dashing from

one nut to another, freezing every ten seconds in melodramatic attitudes of exaggerated alarm, then bounding on again; the nuts were almost too big for them to handle, some had to be rolled along the ground. They were burying their booty, Miss Norah noticed, in a hollow at the foot of the tree; doing half my work for me, she thought, I can just pick them out of there, will Maud ever let me out, that is! And then she thought it was rather a shame that the squirrels should have all their work for nothing; they would be aghast when they came back to find their winter supply gone. But someone had said that squirrels have very poor memories; half the time they forget where they have hidden their nuts, or the hoards are found, accidentally, by some other squirrel.

Glancing at the big black clock on the mahogany bureau, Miss Norah switched on her radio, keeping the volume low. The radio had been acquired secretly from old Biddy in exchange for a man's motheaten fur coat: Maud knew nothing about it and would raise Cain if she ever discovered it, or that the fur coat was missing; Maud thought that a radio was the voice of the Evil Principle.

". . . Eight o'clock news," the voice said. "The strike of French air-traffic controllers is now in its . . . An earthquake in Yugoslavia has destroyed thousands of . . . An oil slick two miles long is drifting . . . A British cabinet minister has been charged with . . . A new Russian space satellite is about to be . . . A Nobel prize winner has fallen from . . . A truck stolen from a Dublin park is being urgently sought by police. The truck contains a load of poisoned walnuts intended to kill the squirrels in the parks; the nuts could be extremely dangerous if they fell into the wrong hands. The registration of the lorry is . . . Anybody seeing it or with information as to its whereabouts should contact the Dublin police. . . . And now, the weather: today will be fine and warm after an early mist."

Wicked shame to poison the poor squirrels, thought Miss Norah, switching off the radio and twisting her hair into a knot which she skewered with an ivory prong. Squirrels do ever so much less harm than humans. Taking a few nuts; poor dumb animals. Whereas humans kidnap each other, let loose oil slicks, shoot those things off into space without proper control; they leave each other stranded in airports; they are downright nasty to each other most of the time. Give me squirrels, I'd say.

She walked from the room, after flinging the covers negligently over her bed, down the ancient, shallow staircase, across the stone-flagged hall, and into the kitchen, where her sister Maud was already drinking tea and eating soda bread. The two sisters had a bedroom each and lived all day in the kitchen; the rest of the large house, half manor, half farm, was left unused. Its rooms were filled with handsome furniture slowly becoming mildewed with damp. The house was called Castle Dore. An old woman, Biddy, came two or three times a week from the village five miles off to help the sisters, but she was almost as frail as they, and next time she fell off her bicycle, she'd said, she'd have to stay at home. In any case, washing sheets and baking soda bread was about as much as she ever achieved.

Miss Maud was thin, sharp, and angry-looking where Miss Norah was round, crumpled, and vague. Maud had a mad fanatic eye and a down-drawn mouth. Countess Sweeney her name really was, believe it or not, for many years ago she had married Count Dermot Sweeney. Count Dermot had been seventy at the time and Maud twenty; all the grand people round about said it was a scandalous match, for she was the scullery maid at Castle Dore, which the Count had bought when he made a fortune and came back from Hollywood to live in Ireland. His fortune had come mostly from a dance he invented called the Sewanee Glide; but people in Ireland called it the Sweeney Glide. You tucked your elbows in to your sides, spread out your fingers, wriggled your wrists, and minced along that way swaying your hips. Oh it was a most disgraceful dance; no nice girl would be seen doing it. A lot of the other sort enjoyed it, however; and in America it caught on like wildfire. So Dermot Sweeney became a rich man and later on was made a Count of the Holy Roman Empire, which many people thought he did not deserve, though it was true he had written many serious songs such as "The Deep Heart's Core," and "Una from Kildoon," "Mary from Clare" and "My Little Erin Lily," which were universally popular and admired. Money sometimes came in, even now, from those songs, but more especially from the Sweeney Glide, which was still performed in clubs and halls where they practiced Old Tyme Dancing.

Naturally the sisters were glad of the money coming in, little enough though it was, for Castle Dore had proved a mortally expensive house to keep up. The roof leaked, and the doors warped, one thing after another. And Maud refused to move; she said it wouldn't be respectful. She would have preferred the Sweeney Glide forgotten. None of the neighbors would call on them, the grand people from the big houses who in Dermot's lifetime were glad enough to accept his subscriptions for their hospitals and charities. He and his dance were too vulgar to be remembered now with anything but distaste. So Norah and Maud saw no one but each other; they had paid their brothers' fares to America long ago. Sometimes there would be a postcard from Houston or St. Louis. And, at Christmas, boxes of mixed nuts.

"A beautiful day," Miss Norah said, pouring herself a cup of black stewed tea. It had an iridescent scum on it like pond water. She buttered a bit of soda bread and sat down at the untidy kitchen table on which lay newspapers, lamps, cabbages, mousetraps, flypaper, string, onions, a bible, a rosary, and baskets of potatoes.

"A beautiful day to pick blackberries."

Cunning Miss Norah thought she would lead around to the walnuts by stages.

"No time to go out gadding," said Miss Maud sourly.

"You're all behind on your curtain. You must set to it directly you've finished that bit of bread."

"Yerrah, Maud, what's the good of going on and on with the old curtains, will you be telling me?"

"It shows consideration for the dead."

"And why should we consider him when he never considered us? And when nobody else does?"

"Mind your tongue. Norah, will you! Maybe he hears you this very minute!"

If he does, I hope his ears would burn, thought Miss Norah rebelliously, but she kept her thoughts to herself, and afterwards sat with her sister, sulky but submissive, at a smaller table they had hauled into the great kitchen, where, day after day, they performed their unending task of mending all the aged brocade curtains in the house, quilting the rotten and splitting fabric with hundreds of rows of tiny parallel stitches.

While they sewed Miss Maud talked about their ungrateful ne'er-do-well brothers and the insolent airs of the neighbors who thought themselves too grand to come calling or so much as pass the time of day with the sisters from Castle Dore.

" 'Tis on the other side of their faces they'll be laughing after we're dead and gone, when they find we've left Castle Dore for a madhouse."

"I only hope the poor simpletons enjoy it here," Miss Norah observed doubtfully, biting off a thread.

During the forty years that she had lived in Castle Dore, she had come to the conclusion that it was a sad old place.

Two hours later she said, all of a sudden (but it had taken her weeks to muster up the courage):

"Maud, couldn't we have a bit of music, now, to beguile the long, weary hours of stitching?"

Maud stared at her.

"*Music?* Are you clean daft yourself, woman?—What do you mean, music?"

"I only thought—we could put one of his records on the

machine. Sure, himself wouldn't be minding! He might be pleased, even, that we'd had the thought."

She nodded through the door to the huge dining room beyond, where, on a massive mahogany sideboard now blue with damp, stood an equally massive old phonograph, in a solid wooden chest, with a winding handle and a hinged lid. The lid was up and showed a trumpet-shaped amplifier; but the phonograph had not been used for years; the red velvet turntable was gray with dust. A pile of brown paper-wrapped records lay beside the machine.

Maud went perfectly white. Her eyes blazed.

"Are you clean crazy, Norah? That you should *dare*, even to have had the thought! Never let me hear you utter it again!"

"Why?" demanded Norah obstinately.

"Because! Because it's best not to be thinking of that heathen music!"

Norah did not remind her that the scanty takings from the heathen music paid for their potatoes and cabbage and flour and the thread with which they were darning the curtains. She said wistfully, "Biddy was telling me that in Dublin these days they do be playing and dancing to those tunes again; doing the Sweeney Glide, even!"

"And what would Biddy be knowing about Dublin—she that never set foot on its streets in her whole life?"

Miss Maud had stayed a night in Dublin once, to see a lawyer about the Count's will, which turned out to bequeath a whole lot of money that he had already spent; Miss Norah had never been there. She replied placidly, "Biddy heard it on the radio."

"The radio! Another devil's invention. Be silent, now, let you, and allow me to get on with my work in peace."

The morning went by, and the afternoon.

At last Miss Norah, stretching her stiff back, peered into the water pail and said:

"I doubt Biddy's not coming this day. She was saying last time, if she fell off her bicycle she didn't know if she would be coming again. Had I not best be fetching in another pailful, Maud, from the well?"

It was eighteen months since the water pipes in Castle Dore had ceased to function; Mikey Meagher the plumber had promised to come, but he was a busy man with many commitments: he had not yet found time.

"Oh, very well," agreed Maud ungraciously. "And you could pull a pair of turnips for soup while you're at it."

"And will I not pick up a few walnuts? 'Tis a terrible shame the squirrels would be getting them all, the creatures."

"Ah, Norah, leave over worrying about the walnuts, will you? They'll keep a while yet," said Maud, who was given to aggravating spells of self-mortification. Later, Norah knew, she would be cantankerous because the walnuts were all gone.

Delighted, anyway, at her spell of liberation, Norah hurried out with the clanking pail. But when she had left it, slopping, by the back door and carried away the garden fork for the turnip digging, she did not go directly to the vegetable patch, but instead found an old leather bag that himself had used for fishing and made her way over the limp warm autumn grass to the walnut tree.

As she moved about in the last of the sun, enjoyably collecting the nuts in their bruised green rinds, which immediately stained her fingers brown, she muttered to herself.

"Ah, she's a tyrant entirely, that one! Curtains, curtains, curtains, the everlasting day! And I with a backbone fit to break in two, and me eyes going back on me, and what good is it at all, tell me? When we're dead and gone the curtains will be falling to tatters innyhow, for never tell me they'll set the poor dafties to stitching them. And not even a note of music to beguile the tedious time! And all himself's tunes lying dumb there in the paper. One of these days I'll be telling her. . . . One of these days I'll be giving her the rough side of my tongue."

Knowing this would never happen, she thought about it pleasurably as she slipped the dank green globes into her bag.

"Ye mean-minded slave-driving bitch, I'll say to her. Ah, I'll not mince my words! Ye wouldn't let me marry Donny Creagan, the time when he offered for me, because, ye said, it would be marrying below our station. Station! What station do I have here, answer me that? 'Tis the station of an unpaid kitchen maid. And now Donny's been wed to Rose Cormack these thirty years, and eighteen grandchildren, if not more, and they off to Newport, Rhode Island to stay with the eldest. And what pleasure or comfort do I have the livelong day? Walnuts!"

She hoisted the bagful, which by now weighed almost as much as she could carry, and nodded upwards to a couple of squirrels, who were watching her with hostility from high in the tree.

"All right, ye little varmints! Ye can have the lave of them, and don't give yourselves the stomachache with overeating!"

Chuckling, she trudged over to an ivy-grown wall which concealed the farm buildings. These, like the house, like the aged, dying trees in the park, like the overgrown gardens, were suffering from fifty years of neglect and disuse. Roofs had caved in; doors sagged from rusty hinges; old carts rotted away where they stood.

It was a surprise, therefore, to Miss Norah, carrying her bag into the cart shed, to find a fairly new truck snugly tucked into a corner behind an ancient haywagon.

For a moment she thought, Mikey Meagher has come to mend the pipes at last! but then she remembered that Mikey had the use of his uncle's Land-Rover, and, anyway, always left it in front of the house with the engine running. Whereas this was a gray truck and had been carefully stowed where it looked as if someone hoped it would not be seen.

Muttering to herself in wonder, Miss Norah squinted into the driver's cab.

"And why in the name of mystery would anyone be leaving a truck in our shed, now? And where's the fellow that drove it here, and isn't it a strange thing now he wouldn't be coming to the house for a cup of tea and a friendly word?"

Peering shortsightedly, she passed along the side of the vehicle and stood on tiptoe to investigate its load. This, whatever it might be, was contained in blue plastic sacks, the kind used by farmers for fertilizer and animal food. But there was something else too.

"Ah, bless them, the peaceful pair," breathed Miss Norah, gazing with sentimental admiration at the two long-haired boys lying on the blue sacks. "And aren't they the living spit of a pair of holy angels?"

In this she did the boys more than justice. One of them was good-looking enough, with yellow hair and a round-faced, red-cheeked, plowboy's charm, but the other, even when sleeping, had something lopsided about his face, a birth defect, perhaps, which dragged down one side of his mouth. Poor gossoon, thought Miss Norah sympathetically, and his brother such a handsome one; but perhaps his is the better nature.

She was moving away to let them have their sleep out, but the shed was full of old rusty implements, and she knocked over a shoulder yoke as she stepped backwards. It fell, clattering, against an empty churn and both boys shot upright on the instant.

"Jeeze! 'Tis one o' the old catamarans!" the handsome one hissed.

"You said they never came out here!"

"Jamesy Phelan said so. How was I to know she'd come today?"

"Ye're kindly welcome, boys," Miss Norah told them timidly, for now they were awake they looked a good deal less angelic, indeed, if the truth be known, somewhat threatening, as they stared down at her from the side of the truck. The round-faced one was scowling, and him with the twisted mouth had a look that was downright nasty.

"You'd best not tell anyone you saw us," said the ugly boy in a tone of menace.

"Deed, an' I'll not," promised Miss Norah cheerfully. "For the matter of that, who would I be telling? There's only my sister, and she too wrapped in her own concerns to hear a single word I say. So let you be easy, now, the pair of ye."

This did not wholly disperse the ugly boy's suspicions.

"If you should ever breathe a word—we'll come back in the dark of the night and slit your tripes—"

"Ah, now, shet up, will ye, Brian," said the handsome boy. "She'll not tell on us, she said so! We'll be gone by dark, Missis, we're just resting, d'ye see, on our way, taking the truck down to a fella we know in County Cork—"

"Will you hold your whisht, you eejit," growled Brian, giving him a kick. "No need to shout our news to the whole countryside—"

"County Cork, as I was saying," the handsome boy went on equably. Even Miss Norah could see he was lying. "And what harm in that?—I suppose ye wouldn't have a cake or a loaf and a pot of tea ye could spare, now, Missis?" he added in a wheedling tone, giving her a hopeful smile. His eyes were bright blue—almost the blue of Donny's when he had come courting.

"Ah, I daren't," she said sadly. "There's my sister in the house, d'ye see. She'd want to know what was I doing with it."

"Will she come out here?" They looked anxious.

"Not she, don't fret yourselves: she bides at her stitching all the time that the light lasts," Miss Norah reassured them. Then she had a bright idea. "I could be bringing ye some boiled potatoes now—I take a potful to the hens at this time of the evening—"

She did not mention that the potatoes were rotten, second-crop ones, bought cheap from a forage firm.

"Potatoes! We aren't pigs," the ugly one grumbled.

"That's all there is," Miss Norah said peaceably. "Unless you have a fancy for a few walnuts?" She held wide the straps of the leather bag to show its contents. Inexplicably, this seemed to cause the boys great amusement.

"Walnuts! Oh, by the holy pike, *walnuts!* Thank you, Missis, but we have a sight too many walnuts as it is."

"Merciful heavens, what ails ye now, boys?" Miss Norah inquired, greatly puzzled, though pleased, too, at seeing them fall about with laughter.

"Our boss, ye see, was telling us to bring down this truck," explained the handsome one, wiping his eyes. "Take the gray truck at the extremity of the row, says he, for 'tis all loaded up with ball bearings and nuts and bolts as there's a fella down south will give us three hundred for, and another five for the truck yet. But after we get it out here and take a look, what do we find? Devil a nut or a bolt—"

"There's *nuts* enough," put in Brian glumly.

"Arrah, that's so! Twenty sacks of walnuts—enough to make toffee for all the kids in the country—"

"Sacks of *walnuts?*" A vague alarm—a vague recollection—began to stir in the hazy depths of Miss Norah's mind. Walnuts—a truck?—a gray truck? Absently she moved to the tailboard where she could see the registration; then she let out a little whimper of dismay. "*Walnuts?* Ye've not eaten any of them, boys?"

"Not us," Brian said, sour. "Nuts? Is it apes you think we are? But I sure could do with a plate of bacon and eggs—"

"Then don't ye touch these nuts!" shrilled Miss Norah with such impressive emphasis that they gazed at her in surprise. "Why, didn't I hear it this very day on the blessed radio? Every last nut of them is filled up with stricknin poison, enough to put the whole of Dublin city under—they'd kill you as dead as Nebuchadnezzar!"

"Poison?"

"For the squirrels in the parks. They do be poisoning the squirrels—though what harm the poor little creatures have done, only the Lord in his mercy knows—"

It took a while for Miss Norah's exhortations to capture the boys' belief. When the truth had filtered through, they laughed even louder than when she had offered them her walnuts.

"Say now, Tony, did ye ever hear the like? A whole truckload of poisoned walnuts, isn't that grand entirely? Pity we didn't know that back there in the city, we could have left a handful or so for old Dooley at the Mourne Street School—"

"Just what I was thinking! And a basketful for my granda," Tony agreed, wiping his eyes. "Anything to help that one out o' the world—"

"The boss'll never credit they're poisoned. He'll sell them to some supermarket. Jay—then just think of the fatalities!"

They dug each other in the ribs, thinking about it.

"You must not let him have them, indeed you mustn't!" declared Miss Norah, uncertain whether to take them seriously. "You had far best leave them here."

The boys glanced at each other.

"Old Skin-an'-Bone won't want them, and that's a fact!" the ugly boy said pensively. "There can't be many loads of poisoned nuts in the country—they'd be easy traced. And who'd want 'em?"

"Should we not try one on something—to see are they really poisoned? Have ye any stray dog around here, Missis, that needs putting away?"

"Never! The idea!"

"Or a rat, now? There must be rats in the barn?"

"They'd not come out while ye sat here waiting for them."

Brian, however, insisted on scattering a handful of nuts over the dusty earth floor of the cart shed and cracking some of them with a shovel. While he was doing this, the church clock of Kilvarna, across the fields, chimed six o'clock.

"Murder!" exclaimed Tony. "Is it that late already? We must have slept like the dead. Come on Brian, leave fooling—'tis two hours after we should have been away. Now, Missis—ye won't tell on us, will ye?" he added beguilingly to Miss Norah.

"Not if ye leave the nuts here, the way I can be sure you won't be poisoning half the countryside."

"Ah, well; maybe 'tis better so. Where will ye have them now?"

"Ye can put them in the old cesspool behind the barn," replied Miss Norah, who had been giving it some thought. "There's little enough harm they can be doing there."

The cesspool must have been very deep once; it was still a visible depression in the ground. Backing the truck as she directed, they tipped the tailboard so as to slide the plastic sacks down among the giant nettles and hemlock which bore witness to the fertility engendered by previous inmates of Castle Dore. Then, waving cheerfully, the boys righted the tail again and drove off in the gathering dusk, down the back drive, between the two rows of untrimmed shaggy elms.

Miss Norah wandered back thoughtfully to the cart shed and studied the tire marks on the dusty floor. Maud would be crazy-mad wondering where she had got to all this while; but such a rare bit of company, of conviviality, did not come her way twice in a twelve-month if that—she needed time to savor the pleasure of the event. That fair one now, bless him—he had a real look of Donny, in those far-off days when he used to come around courting—and the sly, inveigling way with him too, the creature! As for the other—'twas a shame his face was not right, the poor boy—but no doubt he'd grow into a decent enough man by and by, once he'd got over the wild ways of youth—

She walked to the corner where she had first seen them—and there stopped, rooted, with her mouth open. For a great gray rat, bold as brass, had come out of some cranny while she was off showing the boys where to dump their load, and must have eaten one of the poisoned nuts. Or several. And now the creature was feebly kicking and squealing in its last death agonies—a most disgusting spectacle.

"Lord forgive us all! Will ye believe it now?" whispered Miss Norah. "Will ye ever look at that?"

Up to now, the poison had been a kind of fairytale to her—

though one to be respected. At this moment it became real.
" 'Tis notable stuff, so it is. Ungovernable, I'd say."

And then she thought, providence must have intended some
use for it—or why bring it here?

For a few minutes more she stood staring intently at the
dead rat and the nuts strewn over the floor. Then, carefully,
she gathered up half a dozen of the unbroken ones, and put
them in her apron pocket.

Back at the house, a scolding awaited her.

She bore it patiently.

"Ah, bless us, Maud, and wasn't there the biggest old monster of a dead rat ye ever saw and it floating in the well? And I
having the worst trouble in the world fishing it out? And then
being under the necessity of going to the spring—for we
couldn't be using the well water till it cleared? I'll show ye the
rat if ye don't believe me—"

"And why would I wish to see the ugly thing?" demanded
Maud angrily.

"Will I boil ye an egg, now, for your tea, or maybe two,
after all that waiting?" suggested Norah cunningly.

"Quiet, woman! You know well I never touch flesh or fowl.
Bring out a couple of carrots from the pantry—and an apple—
and a walnut or two—I saw ye, from the window, picking
them up—ye can't fool *me*—"

A couple of hours later when Miss Maud, dead as a doornail,
lay doubled up on the stone floor of the hallway, where she
had staggered in her last convulsions, Miss Norah lit a couple
of candles. Later, she would lay her sister out suitably, and call
the doctor and the priest. But not just yet.

She bore the candles into the dining room and set them on
the sideboard. Then she wound the handle, as she had been
doing in her imagination these many years, put a record on
the velvet turntable, and carefully, attentively, moved the
heavy tone arm across, turning over the head so that the needle hit the record, which had already begun spinning.

She had watched himself doing it once or twice, back there, in those times when she was a young slip of sixteen, fetched up to the house as company for her sister; she remembered the process exactly.

Then, elbows in to her sides, wrists pliant, hands extended, fingers flexing, hips revolving, and humming happily to herself, she began to dance the Sweeney Glide. And thought, wonderingly to herself, as she danced, of the power conferred on her by those sacks of nuts out there behind the barn. All the people who had slighted, spited, scorned, ostracized, rebuffed the sisters. She had them at her mercy now, if she so chose! I could kill the whole country, did I wish, she thought. Or shall I let the poor creatures be?

She sang in a cracked old voice:

> "This is how we do it, darlin', sliding side by side
>   Every morning, every evening,
>   Doing the Sweeney Glide."

She danced on, until the raucous, rhythmic music died away.

She Was Afraid of Upstairs

My cousin Tessie, that was. Bright as a button, she was, good as gold, sweet as sugar. And clever, too. Read anything she would, time she were five. Papers, letters, library books, all manner of print. Delicate little thing, peaky, not pretty at all, but, even when she was a liddle un, she had a way of putting things into words that'd surprise you. "Look at the sun a-setting, Ma," she'd say. "He's wrapping his hair all over his face." Of the old mailman, Jumper, on his red bike, she said he was bringing news from Otherwhere. And a bit of Demarara on a lettuce leaf—that was her favorite treat—a sugarleaf, she called it. "But I haven't been good enough for a sugarleaf to-day," she'd say. "Have I, Ma?"

Good she mainly was, though, like I said, not a bit of harm in her.

But upstairs she would not go.

Been like that from a tiny baby, she had, just as soon as she could notice anything. When my Aunt Sarah would try to carry her up, she'd shriek and carry on, the way you'd think she was being taken to the slaughterhouse. At first they thought it was on account she didn't want to go to bed, maybe afraid of the dark, but that weren't it at all. For she'd settle to bed anywhere they put her, in the back kitchen, the broom closet under the stairs, in the lean-to with the boiler, even in the coal shed, where my Uncle Fred once, in a temper, put her cradle. "Let her lie there," he said. "If she won't sleep up in the bedroom, let her lie there."

And lie there she did, calm and peaceable, all the livelong night, and not a chirp out of her.

My Aunt Sarah was fair put about with this awkward way of Tessie's, for they'd only the one downstairs room, and, evenings, you want the kids out of the way. One that won't go upstairs at night is a fair old problem. But, when Tessie was three, Uncle Fred and Aunt Sarah moved to Birmingham, where they had a back kitchen and a little bit of garden, and in the garden my Uncle Fred built Tessie a tiny cabin, not much bigger than a packing case it wasn't, by the back kitchen wall, and there she had her crib, and there she slept, come rain, come snow.

Would she go upstairs in the day?

Not if she could help it.

"Run up, Tessie, and fetch me my scissors—or a clean towel —or the hairbrush—or the bottle of camomile," Aunt Sarah might say, when Tessie was big enough to walk and run errands. Right away, her lip would start to quiver, and that frantic look would come in her eye. But my Aunt Sarah was not a one to trifle with. She'd lost the big battle, over where Tessie was to sleep. She wasn't going to have any nonsense in small ways. Upstairs that child would have to go, whether she liked it or not. And upstairs she went, with Aunt Sarah's eye on her, but you could hear, by the sound of her feet, that she was having to drag them, one after the other; they were so unwilling it was like hauling rusty nails out of wood. And when she was upstairs, the timid tiptoeing, it was like some wild creature, a squirrel or a bird that has got in by mistake. She'd find the thing, whatever it was, that Aunt Sarah wanted, and then, my word, wouldn't she come dashing down again as if the cops were after her, put the thing, whatever it might be, into her mum's hands, and then out into the garden to take in big gulps of the fresh air. Outside was where she liked best to be; she'd spend whole days in the garden, if Aunt Sarah let her. She had a little patch, where she grew lettuce and cress, Uncle Fred got the seeds for her, and then people used to give her bits of slips and flower seeds; she had a real gift for getting things to grow. That garden was a pretty place, you couldn't see the ground for the greenstuff and flowers. Narcissus, bluebells, sweetpeas, marigolds.

Of course the neighbors used to come and shove their oar in. Neighbors always will. "Have a child that won't go upstairs? I'd not allow it if she was mine," said Mrs. Oakley that lived over the way. "It's fair daft if you ask me. *I'd* soon leather her out of it." For in other people's houses Tessie was just the same—when she got old enough to be taken out to visit. Upstairs she would not go. Anything but that.

Of course they used to try and reason with her, when she was old enough to express herself.

"Why won't you go, Tessie? What's the matter with upstairs? There's nothing bad up there. Only the beds and the chests of drawers. What's wrong with that?"

And Aunt Sarah used to say, laughing, "You're nearer to heaven up there."

But no, Tessie'd say, "It's bad, it's bad! Something bad is up there." When she was very little she'd say, "Darkwoods. *Darkwoods*" and "Grandfather Moon! I'm frightened, I'm frightened!" Funny thing that, because, of the old moon itself, a-sailing in the sky, she wasn't scared a bit, loved it dearly, and used to catch the silvery light in her hands, if she were out at night, and say it was like tinsel falling from the sky.

Aunt Sarah was worried what would happen when Tessie started school. Suppose the school had an upstairs classroom, then what? But Uncle Fred told her not to fuss herself, not to borrow trouble; very likely the child would have got over all her nonsense by the time she was of school age, as children mostly do.

A doctor got to hear of her notions, for Tessie had the diptheery, one time, quite bad, with a thing in her throat, and he had to come ever so many times.

"This isn't a proper place to have her," he says, for her bed was in the kitchen—it was winter then, they couldn't expect the doctor to go out to Tessie's little cubbyhole in the garden. So Aunt Sarah began to cry and carry on and told him how it was.

"I'll soon make an end of that nonsense," says he, "for now she's ill she won't notice where she is. And then, when she's better, she'll wake up and find herself upstairs, and her phobia will be gone." That's what he called it, a phobia. So he took Tessie out of her crib and carried her upstairs. And, my word, didn't she create! Shruk! You'd a thought she was being skinned alive. Heads was poking out of windows all down the street. He had to bring her down again fast. "Well, she's got a good strength in her; she's not going to die of the diptheery, at all events," says he, but he was very put out, you could see that. Doctors don't like to be crossed. "You've got a willful one there, Missus," says he, and off he goes, in high dudgeon. But he must have told another doctor about Tessie's willfulness, for a week or so later, along comes a Doctor Trossick, a mind doctor, one of them pussycologists, who wants to ask Tessie all manner of questions. Does she remember this, does she remember that, when she was a baby, and *why* won't she go upstairs, can't she tell him the reason, and what's all this about Grandfather Moon and Darkwoods? Also, what about when her Ma and Pa go upstairs; isn't she scared for them too?

"No, it's not dangerous for them," says Tessie. "Only for me."

"But *why* is it dangerous for you, child? What do you think is going to happen?"

"Something dreadful! The worst possible thing!"

Dr. Trossick made a whole lot of notes, asked Tessie to do all manner of tests on a paper he'd brought, and then he tried to make her go upstairs, persuading her to stand on the bottom step for a minute, and then on the next one, and the one after. But by the fourth step she'd come to trembling and shaking so bad, with the tears running down, that he hadn't the heart to force her any farther.

So things stood, when Tessie was six or thereabouts. And

then one day the news came: the whole street where they lived was going to be pulled down. Redevelopment. Rehousing. All the little two-up, two-downs was to go, and everybody was to be shifted to high-rise blocks. Aunt Sarah, Uncle Fred, and Tessie were offered an apartment on the sixteenth floor of a block that was already built.

Aunt Sarah was that upset. She loved her little house. And as for Tessie—"It'll kill her for sure," Aunt Sarah said.

At that, Uncle Fred got riled. He was a slow man, but obstinate.

"We can't arrange our whole life to suit a child," he said. "We've been offered a Council apartment—very good, we'll take it. The kid will have to learn she can't have her own way always. Besides," he said, "there's elevators in them blocks. Maybe when she finds she can go up in an elevator, she won't take on as much as if it was only stairs. And maybe the sixteenth floor won't seem so bad as the first or second. After all, *we'll* all be on one level—there's no stairs in a flat."

Well, Aunt Sarah saw the sense in that. And the only thing she could think of was to take Tessie to one of the high-rise blocks and see what she made of it. Her cousin Ada, that's my Mom, had already moved into one of the tower blocks, so Aunt Sarah took Tessie out in her stroller one afternoon and fetched her over to see us.

All was fine to start with, the kid was looking about her, interested and not too bothered, till the stroller was wheeled into the elevator and the doors closed.

"What's this?" says Tessie then.

"It's an elevator," says Aunt Sarah, "and we're going to see your Auntie Ada and Winnie and Dorrie."

Well, when the elevator started going up, Aunt Sarah told us, Tessie went white as a dishcloth, and time it got up to the tenth, that was where we lived, she was flat on the floor. Fainted. A real bad faint it was, she didn't come out of it for ever so long, and Aunt Sarah was in a terrible way over it.

"What have I done, what have I done to her," she kept saying.

We all helped her get Tessie home again. But after that the kid was very poorly. Brain fever, they'd have called it in the old days, Mom said. Tossing and turning, hot as fire, and delirious with it, wailing and calling out about Darkwoods and Grandfather Moon. For a long time they was too worried about her to make any plans at all, but when she begun to mend, Aunt Sarah says to Uncle Fred,

"*Now* what are we going to do?"

Well, he was very put out, natural, but he took his name off the apartment list and began to look for another job, somewhere else, where they could live on ground level. And at last he found work in a little seaside town, Topness, about a hundred miles off. Got a house and all, so they was set to move.

They didn't want to move before Tessie was middling better, but the city council was pushing and pestering them to get out of their house because the whole street was coming down; the other side had gone already, there was just a big huge stretch of gray rubble, as far as you could see, and half the houses on this side was gone too.

"What's *happening?*" Tessie kept saying when she looked out of the window. "What's happening to our world?"

She was very pitiful about it.

"Are they going to do that with my garden too?" she'd say. "All my sweetpeas and marigolds?"

"Don't you worry, dearie," says Aunt Sarah. "You can have a pretty garden where we're going."

"And I won't have to sleep upstairs?"

"No, no, Dad'll fix you a cubbyhole, same as he has here."

So they packed up all their bits and sticks, and they started off. Sam Whitelaw lent them his grocery van for the move, and he drove it too.

It was a long drive—over a hundred miles, and most of it through wild, bare country. Tessie liked it all right at first, she stared at the green fields and the sheep, she sat on Aunt Sarah's lap and looked out of the window, but after a few hours, when they were on the moor, she began to get very poorly, her head was as hot as fire and her hands too. She didn't complain, but she began to whimper with pain and weakness, big tears rolled down, and Aunt Sarah was bothered to death about her.

"The child wasn't well enough to move yet. She ought to be in a bed. What'll we do?"

"We're only halfway, if that," says Mr. Whitelaw. "D'you want to stop somewhere, Missus?"

The worst of it was, there weren't any houses around there —not a building to be seen for miles and miles.

On they went, and now Tessie was throwing herself from side to side, delirious again, and crying fit to break her mother's heart.

At last, ahead of them—it was glimmery by then, after sunset of a wintry day—they saw a light and came to a little old house, all by itself, set a piece back off the road against a wooded scawp of hill.

"Should we stop here and see if the folk will help us?" suggested Mr. Whitelaw, and Aunt Sarah says, "Oh, yes. Yes! Maybe they have a phone and can send for a doctor. Oh I'm worried to death," she says. "It was wicked to move the child so soon."

The two men went and tapped at the door and somebody opened it. Uncle Fred explained about the sick child, and the owner of the house—an old, white-haired fellow, Aunt Sarah said he was—told them, "I don't have a phone, look'ee, I live here all on my own. But you're kindly welcome to come in and put the poor little mawther in my bed."

So they all carried Tessie in among them—by that time she was hardly sensible. My poor aunt gave a gasp when she stepped inside, for the house was really naught but a barn or shippen, with a floor of beaten earth and some farm stuff, wagons and carts and piles of turnips.

"Up here," says the old man, and shows them a flight of stone steps by the wall.

Well, there was nothing for it; up they had to go.

Above was decent enough, though. The old fellow had two rooms, fitted up as bedroom and kitchen, with an iron cooking stove, curtains at the windows, and a bed covered with old blankets, all felted-up. Tessie was almost too ill to notice where she'd got to. They put her on the bed, and the old man went to put on a kettle—Aunt Sarah thought the child should have a hot drink.

Uncle Fred and Mr. Whitelaw said they'd drive on in the van and fetch a doctor, if the old man could tell them where to find one.

"Surely," says he, "there's a doctor in the village—Wootten-under-Edge, five miles along. Dr. Hastie—he's a real good un, he'll come fast enough."

"Where is this place?" says Uncle Fred. "Where should we tell him to come?"

"He'll know where it is," says the old man. "Tell him Darkwoods Farm."

Off they went, and the old man came back to where Aunt Sarah was trying to make poor Tessie comfortable. The child was tossing and fretting, whimpering and crying that she felt so ill, her head felt so bad!

"She'll take a cup of my tansy tea. That'll soothe her," said the old man, and he went to his kitchen and brewed up some green drink in an old blue and white jug.

"Here, Missus," said he, coming back. "Try her with a little of this."

A sip or two did seem to soothe poor Tessie, brung her to herself a bit, and for the first time she opened her eyes and took a look at the old man.

"Where is this place?" she asked. She was so weak, her voice was no more than a thread.

"Why, you're in my house," said the old man. "And very welcome you are, my dear!"

"And who are you?" she asked next.

"Why, lovey, I'm old Tom Moon the shepherd—old Grandfather Moon. I lay you never expected you'd be sleeping in the moon's house tonight!"

But at that, Tessie gave one screech and fainted dead away.

Well, poor Aunt Sarah was that upset, with trying to bring Tessie around, but she tried to explain to Mr. Moon about Tessie's trouble, and all her fears, and the cause of her sickness.

He listened, quiet and thinking, taking it all in.

Then he went and sat down by Tessie's bed, gripping hold of her hand.

She was just coming around by then; she looked at him with big eyes full of fright, as Aunt Sarah kneeled down by her other side.

"Now, my dearie," said Mr. Moon, "you know I'm a shepherd; I never hurt a sheep or a lamb in my life. My job is to look after 'em, see? And I'm certainly not a-going to hurt *you*. So don't you be frit now—there's nothing to be frightened of. Not from old Grandfather Moon."

But he could see that she was trembling all over.

"You've been scared all your life, haven't you, child?" said he gently and she nodded, Yes.

He studied her then, very close, looked into her eyes, felt her head, and held her hands.

And he said, "Now, my dearie, I'm not going to tell ye no lies. I've never told a lie yet—you can't be lying to sheep or lambs. Do ye believe that I'm your friend and wish you well?"

Again she gave a nod, even weaker.

He said, "Then, Tessie my dear, I have to tell you that you're a-going to die. And *that's* what's been scaring you all along. But you were wrong to be in such a fret over it, lovey, for there's *naught to be scared of*. There'll be no hurt, there'll be no pain, it be just like stepping through a door. And I should know," he said, "for I've seen a many, many sheep and lambs taken off by weakness or the cold. It's no more than going to sleep in one life and waking up in another. Now do ye believe me, Tessie?"

Yes, she nodded, with just a hint of a smile, and she turned her eyes to Aunt Sarah, on the other side of the bed.

And with that, she took and died.

The Birthday Party

"Time for your music lesson, Juniper," said Mrs. Campbell. She had to repeat the sentence three times before it had any effect. Then, slowly, with a scowl, Juniper Campbell laid aside the magazine she was reading, found her music case, put on her jacket, and prepared to go off to the house of Mrs. Holam, who gave piano lessons and lived two streets away.

"I'd hardly have thought you needed gloves. It's very warm —as you'd know if you ever put your nose outside the house, instead of reading comics right through the day," said Mrs. Campbell and received another scowl from her daughter. Juniper did not answer but trudged toward the front door as if she were setting off for a labor camp in Siberia.

"She's only wearing gloves because they're the new ones Aunt Cecile sent her," said Charley, Juniper's younger brother. He too got a look that boded him little good when Juniper came back from her lesson. Undisturbed by this, he went on, as the door slammed behind his sister, "I think Aunt Cecile's a horrible lady. Why do we have to call her aunt when she isn't one really?"

"Because she is one of your father's most paying clients."

In fact Mrs. Campbell also thought Aunt Cecile—Lady Walravens—a perfectly horrible person, but what could you do? Part of her horribleness consisted of a permanent dislike for whatever husband and house she happened to have at the moment and a wish for new ones; the second part of this wish came in very handy for Mr. Campbell, an architect, who occupied a large part of his time in discovering new houses for Aunt Cecile and then completely remodeling them to her peevish requirements. At the end of six months she would find fault with everything in them and demand something different.

"*Why* does Aunt Cecile give presents to Juniper and not to the rest of us?"

"She took a fancy to Juniper as a baby; I suppose you could call her a kind of unofficial godmother."

"*I* don't know how *any*body could take a fancy to Juniper at *any* age," Charley gloomily remarked.

His mother agreed with him. "Juniper's going through an awkward phase," people said, but they had been saying it for years now. In fact, ever since Aunt Cecile, seeing the two-year-old Juniper furiously dash a bowl of prune puree onto a tiled floor, had exclaimed admiringly, "*There's* a child who knows what she likes and what she doesn't. No one's ever going to put anything over on *her*."

No one ever had. And it was then that the present giving had begun: all the presents wholly unsuitable, deplored by Juniper's mother—but, again, what could you do? Juniper herself, needless to say, received the presents with rapture; she would even write thank-you letters to Aunt Cecile without being told to. There had been, when she was six, the miniature power lawn mower, with which she nearly cut off Charley's arm; when she was seven a season ticket to the ballet, which meant that somebody had to take her and fetch her every week (luckily she became bored with ballet halfway through the year); when she was eight, a genuine crocodile-skin handbag, and high-heeled shoes; when she was nine, a watch with real rubies in it; and endless smaller gifts, fans, makeup, huge boxes of chocolates, frilly underwear. "Because *I* didn't have anything like that at her age," Aunt Cecile used to say, and Mrs. Campbell had to suppress the retort "And a good thing too."

The last present had been that absurd pair of elbow-length blue suede gloves, completely unsuitable and unnecessary.

"I'm sure I could play the piano much better if I wore my gloves," said Juniper with a coy smile. "Then my fingers wouldn't slip off the keys."

But Mrs. Holam, who stood no nonsense from anybody, said, "Don't be silly, child; take them off at once and play your scales."

By the end of the lesson Mrs. Holam was in a very bad mood, and Juniper was in a worse one.

"If you don't practice at all, Juniper, it's a perfect waste of my time to teach you."

"No, it jolly well isn't, you get three pounds a lesson," muttered Juniper, spinning herself off the piano stool so that it whirled high up, and the screw would have come right out of its socket if Mrs. Holam hadn't stopped it. She ignored her pupil's retort and said, "I shall expect you to know the minuet *perfectly* next time you come, and you must do at least half an hour's sight reading every day. I'm afraid you are likely to get a very bad report at the end of the term unless you change your habits."

Juniper walked back to the Campbells' house dragging her feet and frowning. But in the mailbox at home she found something that turned her thoughts in a different direction. This was an invitation to Sigrid Smith's birthday party, seven days away.

"Now isn't that nice," said Mrs. Campbell, who preferred a pleasant atmosphere and had noticed her daughter's lowering look. "You'll be able to wear your pink and black paisley and the petticoat and shoes that Aunt Cecile gave you. You ought to take a present, I suppose; what should it be?"

"Why should I have to give *her* anything? She only asks me because she's got to," growled Juniper.

(This was indeed the case: Mrs. Smith, looking at the list, had said, "You can't invite all your class and leave out Juniper Campbell," and Sigrid had said, "Oh, Mom, *must* I? Everybody hates her," and Mrs. Smith had said, "Yes, you must," and Sigrid, writing the name on a card, had grumbled, "She's sure to do something awful and spoil everybody's fun.")

Then Juniper, looking at the invitation again, brightened, and said, "Oh, good, it's on my music-lesson evening; does that mean I can skip horrible Mrs. Holam?"

"No, it certainly doesn't. You know your father wants you to be good at the piano. We'll ask Mrs. Holam if she can kindly change the time, just that once."

However this was not necessary, as Mrs. Holam herself rang up a few days later to say that music lessons must come to a stop for several weeks; her house had been broken into by vandals who, as well as stealing all her portable valuables, had smashed up her piano, her television set, and her tanks of tropical fish.

"Serve her right, beastly old hag," murmured Juniper, but she murmured it under her breath.

"Poor Mrs. Holam!" exclaimed Juniper's mother. "It's too awful—all her nice things. . . . Which reminds me, darling, have you bought a birthday present for Sigrid yet? You haven't? Oh, heavens, you really must get one today. You know how hard it is to find anything nice if you leave it to the last minute. Here's two dollars, go and get something. Oh, and Mrs. Holam said you'd left your blue gloves at her house last week; you had better pick them up while you're out."

"She might have told me sooner! I'd been wondering where they were."

Juniper went round by the piano teacher's house and collected the blue gloves; luckily she was not obliged to say anything to Mrs. Holam, who was busy talking to an insurance agent, and merely indicated where the gloves lay on the hall table. Juniper was, however, able to take a happy and revengeful look at the damaged piano, which seemed to have been totally dismantled. "If it were a loaf it would be bread crumbs!" as the insurance man said. "Lord knows how they managed to do it without waking you."

Juniper pulled on her gloves before going out and closing the door. Just at that moment a police car shot screaming by, and Juniper, who was afraid of loud noises, automatically clapped her blue-covered hands over her ears. The sound from outside was instantly cut off, but, to her surprise, a tiny, insistent buzzing seemed to be coming from the palms of her hands:

"Juniper, listen! Juniper, listen! Juniper, listen to this-s-s-s-s. . . ."

She stood listening in Mrs. Holam's front garden; her face, under the freckles, became pale with excitement, and her eyes became rounder and rounder.

Juniper went along to Woolworth's and bought a paperback about hang-gliding for Sigrid Smith; it cost $1.50; Juniper did not think it particularly likely that Sigrid would be taking up hang-gliding, but that left fifty cents over to buy two chocolate bars for herself.

On the day of the party, rain streamed down all afternoon. This was a pity, since Juniper was deprived of the chance to show off her black and pink paisley as she walked through the streets to Sigrid's house. On the other hand, it made a good reason to wear the suede gloves, which went quite well with her blue-gray gabardine raincoat. Juniper did not expect to enjoy the party, for she hated everybody in her class, and they would all be there. But at least the food would be good; Sigrid's mother was a notable cook. Also Juniper was cheered by the thought that her underwear, stockings, and shoes would be nicer than anybody else's.

There were twenty-five people at the party; the whole class, plus some cousins of Sigrid's.

"Here's Archie," called out a boy called Tony Biretta, catching sight of Juniper. He had a sharp nose and a lot of tightly curled black hair and was the class wit. "Hello, Archie, come to make sure the food's okay?"

Juniper made a face at him—a lightning grimace of hate,

pushing up her mouth, wrinkling her nose, and screwing up her eyes.

"Why did he call her Archie?" softly inquired Mrs. Smith of Sigrid, who was taking people's wet coats and greeting them in the front hall.

"It's short for Archipelago, because her face is all covered with blobs of freckles like a map of islands," explained Sigrid in the same low voice.

"Oh dear! Children are so unkind to each other! Poor little thing."

"She's really a horrible girl, Mother, you'll see," said Sigrid.

First they played Mesmerism, sending people out of the room in turn, deciding on a task for them to do, and then humming loud when they went wrong, softly when they were getting warmer, until, without being told, they discovered what they were supposed to do. This wasn't a bad game; Juniper quite enjoyed it until her own turn came, when the others had chosen a very complicated task for her: she had to take a red book from a shelf, find a particular page, and read aloud a certain line from it. She made a hopeless muddle of this, not getting anywhere near doing the right thing, took a long time over it, and a boy called Sid Monk was heard to mutter "Stupid lump."

"Stupid lump yourself!" flashed Juniper. "What *you* had to do was a lot easier!"

"Let's have another game," quickly suggested Sigrid's mother. "How about Dumb Crambo?"

A lot of people didn't know how to play it, but she explained that the players were divided into two teams. Each team had to think of a word and then act, not the word itself, but a whole batch of other words that rhymed with it.

"Okay, let's pick for teams," said Sigrid. "Tony, you pick one side, and Sid, you pick the other."

Of course, Juniper was picked last and went, slowly and sourly, to join Sid's team, which gave her an equally sour welcome.

Dumb Crambo lasted till it was time to eat; everybody was hungry, and as soon as Sigrid's aunt rang the bell, there was a race to the dining room, which was won by Juniper, who had been close to the door. She managed to grab a chair beside a large plate of meringues. These were homemade by Sigrid's mother, large pale golden brown ones, lined with thick cream. Before anybody noticed, Juniper had eaten ten out of the thirty. Then Sigrid's aunt saw what was happening and hissed to her sister, "For heaven's sake, get the meringue plate away from that fat redhaired girl, or there won't be any left. No wonder she's so fat! And what a dress to go with red hair—black and pink!"

There were plenty of other delicious things to eat: mushroom quiche, sausages, brandysnaps, homemade cheese straws, candy-apple pie, and a huge birthday cake. Juniper steadily and methodically packed herself with food. She had no hopes of getting any pleasure from the second half of the party and thought she might as well enjoy herself while she had the chance.

After they ate, Sigrid's mother said they had better play something energetic to start with, as she knew they would all want to settle down and listen to records pretty soon. Most of the guests, including Juniper, would have liked to begin listening at once, but, urged by Mrs. Smith, they reluctantly began on a fan race, divided into the same teams as before, and trying, with fans made of folded paper, to waft a bit of colored tissue across a tape laid in the middle of the floor.

"This is a stupid babies' game," grumbled Juniper. "Paper fans! I've got a real fan at home, made of ivory."

"Oh, we all know you're superior to the rest of us in *every* way," said a girl named Tilly, "but shut up, will you. It's supposed to be a game of skill."

Juniper stuck out her tongue at Tilly and, in the course of the game, contrived to trip her and knock her against the doorpost so that Tilly sprained her finger. Later, Juniper noticed a rather unreliable boy called Adam Parker quietly pocket a silver snuffbox from the mantelpiece. At the end of the game, Juniper marched across the room to Mrs. Smith and announced in ringing tones, "Adam Parker has pinched your silver box. It's in his trouser pocket!"

Curiously enough this revelation, and Adam's disgrace, did not make Juniper any more popular.

Mrs. Smith hastily suggested that they should play a game called How Do You Like Your Neighbor? The guests were to sit in a ring, with one person in the middle, who would then ask one of the sitting players: "How do you like your neighbor?" The person asked could reply, "My neighbors are okay," or, if not satisfied with either or both, could answer, "Not much; I'd rather have Angela than Jim—or Roger and Sue instead of Jinny and Simon." Then, while the changeover was taking place, the middleman would try to grab one of the empty chairs. This, rather a dull game, was made interesting to the rest of the players and painful to Juniper because those who had Juniper beside them were sure to be asked the question by the middleman, and they invariably answered, "I can't stand Juniper," so she was constantly being forced to change seats.

Mrs. Smith had gone off to help her sister tidy up the dishes at the start of this game, but when she came back and saw what was happening, she quickly said that it was time to have a nose-and-matchbox race.

The guests were not too enthusiastic about the nose-and-matchbox idea, but played it with moderate goodwill for ten minutes or so. Then Sigrid said,

"Mom, everyone's tired. We'd like to listen to records now."

"All right, darling, if that's what everybody really wants."

"Oh yes!" everybody shouted in chorus.

Mrs. Smith now felt that she could go away and finish dealing with the dishes, confident that not much could go wrong: everybody was sitting down, nothing was likely to get smashed; and, so long as records were being played, fights between the boys were not likely to break out.

What Mrs. Smith did not know was that, as soon as a rather soft record had been put on, Sid called out,

"Quick, let's play a game of Truth. Tilly, who do you hate worst in this room?"

"Juniper. Adam, who do you think is the rottenest tattletale here?"

"Juniper. Tony, who's the greediest pig in the school?"

"Juniper. Sid, who stinks worst?"

"Juniper. Brenda, who thinks most of herself?"

"Juniper. Clare, who's the ugliest person here?"

"Juniper. . . ."

"Everybody okay?" Mrs. Smith presently said, putting her head around the door. She could hear a good deal of suppressed giggling, but they seemed all right; something fidgety in the atmosphere, though, told Mrs. Smith that it would be a good thing to serve the end-of-party drinks and sandwiches rather sooner than she had intended to.

While the guests were saying their polite thanks, Mrs. Smith noticed that the Campbell child had a rather high color; in fact the gaps between her blotches of freckles seemed to have filled in, so that her face was a kind of mahogany-red all over. Well, it was probably all those meringues she had eaten and serve her right.

"Thank-you-Mrs.-Smith-for-a-nice-party," Juniper said rapidly and slid out through the door before Mrs. Smith could answer, "And do remember me to your mother."

She was one of the first to leave; some of the others stayed much longer.

"Well, I think that was quite a success," Mrs. Smith said firmly to Sigrid, when everybody had gone.

"It would have been if only you hadn't made me ask that ghastly Juniper."

"Darling, you've got to be nice to people; otherwise, how will they ever learn to mix in and be nice themselves?"

"Some people never do learn," said Sigrid darkly. "Oh, look, the horrible beast has left her disgusting gloves behind. Funny she should do that when she brags about them so—*real* suede, elbow length—"

"Well you can take them to school tomorrow and give them back to her. Heavens," said Mrs. Smith yawning, "parties wear me out. . . ."

But Sigrid did not need to return the gloves.

Long after Juniper had gone to bed that night she lay awake, tossing, turning, and raging silently, thinking too late of the retorts she could have made, the cutting things she could have said. Why could she never think of them in time?

Then she heard a soft thump downstairs, as if Toffee the cat had come in through his catdoor.

Juniper sat up in bed alertly. Her door was slightly open, and a ray of moonlight from the window slanted across the floor.

Soon, listening hard, she heard a kind of quiet scurry on the stairs, like the noise made by (for instance) a pair of black widow spiders clambering from step to step.

In a moment the two gloves came through the door, walking delicately on their fingers and thumbs. They crossed the floor, climbed up the legs of the chair, pushed it a little way, fastidiously, from the table, and settled themselves comfortably. They were slightly soiled and smeared; not quite so handsome and new looking as when Aunt Cecile had first presented them; but still Juniper, surveying them, seemed quite satisfied with their appearance.

She slipped the gloves, soiled as they were, onto her hands and cupped her hands over her ears, listening, this time, as if she knew, or hoped, what to expect. And indeed what she heard seemed to amuse her very much; first she chuckled, then she burst out laughing. And then she crossed the room and hung out of the window to see if any red glitter was visible in the sky; but the Smiths' house was around on the other side and she could see nothing at all. But the gloves must know what they are talking about, she thought, and, taking them off, she laid them back carefully on the table, stroking the fingers into position. Then she got into bed.

Like the gloves, she settled herself comfortably and soon sank into a peaceful sleep.

Mousework

A wave swung high and lazily, with a curve like the white breast of a pouter pigeon, swept little Miss Roe clean off the deck of the elderly immigrant ship where she lay sleeping in the sun and sucked her back underwater without any noise or commotion; she vanished among sea thistles, tangled ocean daisies, foam tips crossing this way and that, and the glitter of fins bright as mica. Nobody noticed; she was just a typist, with no relations, on her way to look for a job.

She called for help in her tiny breathless voice and tried to swim, but the waves tired her out with their salty slaps on face and arms; presently she was unconscious, floating and drifting in the teeth of a wandering current that edged her through reefs and slid her up the beach of an island, itself little more than a spit of sand in the enormous shining sea.

After a time Miss Roe recovered consciousness. All she knew at first was the gritty, shifting feel of sand that has had water over it a short time before, warm under her body. Then she raised herself on her forearms and looked about; she saw the gentle slope of the island to her left and the smooth sea, with a curdle of reefs far out, on her right. She brushed off the damp sand and sat up.

There was a salt taste on her lips, not unlike anchovies, not unpleasant; she licked them once or twice and tried to smooth the knots out of her sticky hair before starting off to look for help. She was still wearing her faded old swimsuit, so she was decent enough.

Barefooted she paddled over the hot, yielding sand and

found to her dismay that the island was small, circular, and uninhabited. It consisted of nothing but sandhills, save that in the center there were two springs, one hot, one cold.

The hot spring bubbled and seethed in its own ferment of boiling mud, sinking away as fast as it rose. The cold spring, hardly bigger, nourished a couple of date palms whose long silky leaves, whispering above, cast a small patch of shade into which Miss Roe gratefully dropped.

Clusters of dates hung from the branches: she would not lack food. She ate a few absently, though she was not hungry. Rested, she began again her weary, useless pacing of this simplified horizon. Near the tops of the sandhills she saw small holes, but she prudently avoided them. She had been told that large spiders sometimes live in sand.

Two days passed. Miss Roe was not precisely unhappy, since she had no friends to pine for, but she was lonely and desperately in need of occupation. Never much of a one to read, she was accustomed always to have in hand some piece of knitting or crochet, outside office hours, and the unwonted lack of exercise for her supple fingers irked her terribly. There was no material on the island at all; only the sand and the palm trees whose leaves were too brittle and sharp for satisfactory use.

On the afternoon of the second day Miss Roe was lying by the cool spring, idly watching the water well up and then seep back into the damp sand. Already she was tanned by the sun; her slight body had taken the same color as the sand she lay on, and her unimpressive mouse-colored hair was bleaching to a silvery floss.

She saw two little brown things like bits of fluff approaching.

For one heart-sickening moment she thought that they were spiders, and then, on a breath of relief, perceived that they were in fact mice: small golden-brown mice with bright needlepoint eyes and long, extra-long tails, each ending in a tidy tassel like a miniature feather duster. Normally she was afraid of mice, but these seemed unconnected with the dirty, furtive scufflings behind cheese crock or bread bin which were all her previous experience. They approached with caution, true, but with dignity, pausing at her slightest movement, putting their heads together as if they conferred, and then nimbling on again.

When they were only a couple of feet from her they stopped and went into a great pantomime, nodding their heads, flashing their almost invisible whiskers, gesturing with tiny hands and above all with their elongated mobile tails which whipped to and fro over their backs.

Miss Roe was not at all intelligent, but even she could see that they were communicating with each other and attempting to do so with her.

It took them six months to teach her their language.

The mice lived in tiny cavelike hollows in the sand, shored and lined everywhere inside with slender sea twigs that were polished white as ivory by the passing of countless furry bodies. Their principal food was dried fish flakes, savory, of a soft leaflike consistency, and silver-brown in color. While she was lying unconscious the mice had fed Miss Roe with these; they were highly nutritious and contained vitamin D in large quantities.

It was some time before the mice, whose intelligence was of a high order, realized that Miss Roe was almost totally ignorant about the workings of the civilization from which she had come. At first they questioned her severely on ethics, civics, mathematics, and other topics, but in the end they resigned themselves to the fact that her mind contained little beyond an exhaustive knowledge of knitting patterns and the difference between right and wrong.

They did, however, become very fond of Miss Roe, and when they saw her pining for lack of occupation they started a fur collection, bringing her little heaps of molted mouse down which her skillful fingers twirled into threads and knitted on palm frond needles into various unnecessary articles.

When rescue appeared, in the form of a shabby schooner anchored outside the reef, the mice were saddened by the prospect of Miss Roe's departure.

Tears stood in her guileless eyes too.

"Isn't there anything I can do for you?" she begged. "You've been so kind to me! I could ask them to leave some cheese—or —or books so that you could learn to read—?"

Tass, the senior mouse, looked at her very kindly. His whiskers were gray, his eyes were twinkling. In appearance he was not unlike Einstein.

"The greatest service you can do us," he said, "is to tell no one of our existence. Can you promise that?"

"Of *course* I can!" She scrubbed the shine from her eyes with the back of a brown hand. "Is there truly nothing else?"

"Yes," he said dryly, "you can take those two young hotheads, Afi and Anep, with you and rid our happy republic of a pair of potential troublemakers."

Afi and Anep joyfully accepted the chance to travel. And so, when the crew of the dinghy neared the shore, there was nothing to see but a solitary figure on a bare and uninhabited island. With astonishment they saw Miss Roe, slender and brown, wearing—for this was during the cool equinoctial winds—a bikini and thick sweater of mousewool which many an Italian starlet might have envied. They did not see Afi and Anep, the two young demagogues, whose bright little beady black eyes peered glancingly out through the cable stitch from their snug hiding place inside her big roll collar.

"Cripes," said Ant Arson, "wait till the cap sees this."

"You'd better wait," muttered Singer Jones, "or Cap'll feed you to the tiburones," and he shunted his jaw sideways with a meaningful leer.

The boat's crew seemed haloed with gold to Miss Roe as they pulled towards her. Actually they were as unsavory a load as might have been found anywhere in the South Pacific, and their captain was a fit leader for them.

Valentino McTavish mooched about the ocean with his unshaven crew and his shocking old ship full of unmentionable cargoes, carrying on a dozen illegal trades, engaging in acts of minor piracy when it seemed safe, wanted by the police of every large port but always slipping away just before the net descended.

"Man!" said Valentino McTavish, eyeing Miss Roe with the incredulity of a cat that sees a whole Dover sole laid on its dish. And he helped her over the gunwale.

She noticed first that the *Aurora* seemed full of dirty washing and sardine cans; second, that the captain, though very attentive in a queer way, was not much like Alec Guinness, her ideal of seamanly beauty; third, that the crew, huddled together in the waist, seemed jeeringly in awe of their captain; fourth, that the two totalitarian mice in her collar were becoming restive, possibly because their sharp nostrils detected the odor of proletarian comrades somewhere near at hand.

"I should like to wash my hands, please," she said, and was taken with suspicious promptitude to Valentino's cabin.

The mess and clutter depressed her. She found herself regretting the tidy island and friendly mice, feeling homesick.

She shook Afi and Anep out of her collar, and they rushed greedily about the floor, questing and roving among the discarded underwear and heady, unfamiliar smells, presently making off down holes in the paneling to preach equality and the rights of mice. From time to time they darted joyously back to report on their successes with the ship's rodent population.

"Do be careful!" Miss Roe exclaimed anxiously. "The captain said he was coming back to show me round."

"We won't let him see us!"

They waved their tails in reassurance.

As it happened, they were both sitting on her shoulders, Anep telling her how he had set up committees to form trade unions, Afi reporting a lecture he had delivered to the boiler-room mice on the need for collective ownership of the means of production, when the door opened and Captain McTavish came in. There was just time to fly under her collar once more.

Valentino carried a bottle of palm wine under his arm. He had already drunk half of it. Now he took another swig, put down the bottle, and advanced on Miss Roe in a purposeful manner. His mind was fuddled with drink, a suspicion that his crew were laughing at him, and the need for asserting his authority. A core of anger, mainly at himself, burned in him; his eyes were bloodshot, shamed, and lustful. In many ways he was a piteous object.

To his astonishment, when he laid hold of the petrified Miss Roe, his amatory intentions were interrupted by a series of savage, needle-sharp stabs in his left wrist and right forearm.

He shrieked, clawing at his arms, and shrieked again as, like animated scalpels, the two mice dived for his most vulnerable points.

The crew heard shrieks coming from the cabin, but this was a commonplace. True, the voice sounded like the captain's rather than the girl's, but Valentino was an eccentric, and it would have been the height of indelicacy to intrude—and anyway, more than their lives were worth.

They settled down on the after-hatch, throwing numbered sardine cans for the chance of being next with the girl.

A couple of hours later someone gave a shout and the crew, focusing their eyes as best they could, saw a raft drifting in the *Aurora*'s direction.

"Hey, fellas, there's someone on it."

"It's the crazy Swede. You know? Olaf Myrdal."

"Think we oughta tell Cap?"

"Better not."

"Ah, shucks, we can disturb him by now, surely?"

Ant went down and peered through the cabin keyhole. The yell he let out brought the rest of the crew running, and in panicked incredulity they broke open the door.

Miss Roe was lying on the floor, deeply unconscious. At some distance from her lay a skeleton, white and shining.

It was not until Singer touched the bones and discovered them to be *warm* that real terror set in.

"Where in heck's it *come* from?" bellowed Ant, frightened and sweating, looking for reassurance to the others.

"Where's Cap?"

"But look—look," stuttered Dice Morgan. "Look at that finger."

They looked. On a metacarpal bone shone a band of tarnished gold with a familiar amethyst. The captain had been something of a dandy.

"Good sakes!" breathed Ant. "It's *him*! It *is* Cap!"

Fear soon finds relief in vengeance.

"The girl's done it! Drop her over the side! Feed her to the sharks. She's a witch; she's a Jonah."

Several of the crew were averse to touching Miss Roe at all, but Singer was not so particular, and he dragged her unconscious body on deck.

"Why not put her on the raft?" suggested Dice brilliantly. "We don't want her haunting us. We drop her overboard, the sharks eat her, we get her duppy climbing up the side every night and pulling us in by the ankles. Put her on the raft; let her haunt that loony Swede."

There was a chorus of agreement.

They hailed the raft, which was now floating past their stern.

"Hi, there, you Swede! Will you take a bit of cargo for us?"

The Swede came to the door of his little cabin and surveyed them coldly.

"I wish for nothing that has been on your ship," he said. But already two men had grappled the raft alongside, and two more wrapped Miss Roe's body in a tarpaulin and rolled it over the gunwale. More by luck than judgment it fell on the balsawood deck of the raft.

"Adios, amigos!" shouted the crew of *Aurora*, leaning over the stern rail and waving. "Have a happy honeymoon! Mind she don't turn you to a skellington, Swedy! Disconnecta dem dry bones!"

They drew away.

The Swede reluctantly removed the wrappings from the bundle they had tossed him. When he saw Miss Roe his expression of disapproval deepened. He scooped up a dipper of seawater and dashed it in her face.

Presently she came to, looked around her, and shuddered.

"Did they hurt you?" he said.

Her eyes slowly took him in—his bigness, his slow, gentle movements, his look of rather severe intelligence.

"Who are you? You don't look like those men." She pulled herself to a sitting position. "Am I still on the ship?"

"You are not on the ship, no. They threw you off. Have they injured you?"

Her eyes dilated. "He was going to—that captain! But the mice—it was horrible!" Suddenly she stiffened. "The mice! Afi and Anep—where are they?"

Afi ran from her collar and rubbed affectionately against her chin. She stroked him in relief. The Swede's expression softened as he observed this exchange. But then Miss Roe burst into tears. .

"Do not cry, young lady. I do not know what you were doing on that ship, and I may say frankly that I did not wish for a passenger, especially a female one, but I think you are better off here than there. Wait, and I will make some seaweed tea. My name is Olaf Myrdal," he added with a certain dignity. "You may have heard of me."

"It's my mouse," sobbed poor Miss Roe, unheeding. "The other mouse, Anep! He's been left on that ship. Oh, please, please go back and fetch him."

"Impossible, my dear child," he said gently. "That ship has a far greater command of speed than my raft and, as you can see, it is nearly five miles ahead of us."

Since Miss Roe continued to weep unrestrainedly, he said

after a while, with a slightly admonishing air, "I think you had better tell me about it."

Miss Roe calmed down as she told her story. She couldn't help liking this tall, quiet man with his long sweeping golden beard and his benign expression.

The expression changed to one of qualified surprise as her story proceeded.

"So!" he said. "An island of intelligent mice. I should indeed like to call there. And you can communicate with them?"

"Yes," said Miss Roe, wiping her eyes, "we used to have ever such nice talks in the evening. You'd be surprised what a lot goes through their little heads."

"This mouse you have here is one of them?"

Afi was prospecting busily about the raft, sniffing, tasting, and scrutinizing.

"Can you request your small friend to come here?"

Miss Roe called Afi, who ran confidently up her leg and from the eminence of her wrist looked in a searching manner at Myrdal.

"Does this man come from your country?" he asked Miss Roe, who shook her head. "Excellent," the mouse remarked, "then perhaps he can tell me things you do not know. Ask if in his land they have nationalized the means of production?"

Miss Roe translated this as best she could. Myrdal's eyebrows shot up.

"Doesn't he know?" said Afi, disappointed. "Well, ask him if he is familiar with these concepts: the transition of quantity into quality, the negation of the negation, the interpenetration of opposites?"

"Merciful heavens!" exclaimed the Swede, "to think that I, who have come to sea to escape once and for all from mankind's violence and the conflicts of warring ideologies, should have run up against a Marxist mouse."

Miss Roe, accustomed to the philosophical discussions of her mouse friends, was still unhappy.

"What about poor Anep?" she mourned. "Alone on that ship, among those dreadful men?"

"He will be in no danger. If, as you tell me, he has already organized the ship's mice into trade unions, it is for the men that you should fear. Already they are doomed; already, maybe, they have suffered the fate of their captain. And when the ship reaches port, what then? I believe that you have loosed on mankind, unwittingly, a greater destructive force than the hydrogen bomb. The age of men is ended; that of mice is about to begin."

"Oh dear," said Miss Roe. "Do you think we might have some of that seaweed tea you talked about?" It always took her a little while to absorb a new idea.

"When do *we* reach port?" she asked later, sipping the hot green fluid.

"Never."

"Never? But—"

"Did I not tell you that I came to sea to escape from violence? More than ever now it will be necessary to stay away from the world of men. I have ample resources on the raft— the works of Strindberg, Ibsen, Thomas Hardy, Voltaire, and Shakespeare."

Miss Roe seemed doubtful of these benefits. Then she brightened. "Couldn't we go back to my island?"

"My dear girl, there is nothing I should like better, in due course. But for the moment it would be out of the question. Afi is now a potential menace to the island's peace, since he has had experience of the efficacy of violence. Also—though this is merely a personal consideration—our own lives might be in danger if he were able to tell the other mice about the experiment with Captain McTavish. They might wish to repeat it—especially as you promised not to reveal their existence and have done so."

"Yes—I see." But Miss Roe could hardly believe it of her dear mice.

"Mice do not live long," pronounced Olaf. "We can afford to

drift for a year or two until Afi dies of old age, before we return."

"Poor Afi! He will be rather bored. He was hoping to get to Australia."

"I shall learn his language and teach him Swedish; we shall have philosophical discussions. I shall read him Strindberg, also."

"I suppose you haven't any wool or knitting needles, have you?" said Miss Roe wistfully, feeling a little left out by this program. He shook his head.

"Another thing," he said. "We must be married. For a young girl and a man, even a philosopher like me, to drift about the ocean on a raft without matrimony is not at all seemly."

Married! Miss Roe stared in surprise that approached consternation at this godlike being who spoke the word so matter-of-factly. Never, never, in her wildest dreams. . . .

"But how could we?" she said. "There's no church, no clergyman?"

"Marriage before witnesses is quite correct at sea. Your friend down there is rational—he will do admirably as a witness."

Miss Roe's eyes began to shine. This put a different complexion on things. If she were *married* to this Mr. Myrdal, he would not seem quite so alarming; and she could endure the solemnity of drifting about the Pacific reading Strindberg aloud to a mouse if she were graced with the status of a married woman.

"But mind," he said, "no children!"

"No children?" She was dreadfully cast down. "But if all the world is going to be overrun with mice, surely it's our duty—?"

"My belief is that the human race is due to expire. It shall not be our part to prolong its death throes."

"Oh dear," said Miss Roe again.

The simple marriage ceremony was performed. Afterwards Olaf and Afi, who had taken a great fancy to one another, settled down to a discussion of the philosophy of Kant, conducted by signs.

Miss Roe, now Mrs. Myrdal, stretched out in the rays of the setting sun, chin propped on elbows, and watched them. He was nice, her new husband, she decided; a bit silly with all his fanciful ideas, perhaps, a bit grand and dignified, but ever so kind! And all men had to be learned and managed. It was a shame about the children, though; she had already planned to ask if she couldn't snip off a bit of that long, golden beard. It would knit up lovely into tiny bootees.

Oh well—she stretched and rolled over into the last of the sunshine—there would be plenty of time to persuade him to change his mind.

A Long Way to Swim

A cool dry wind, which had blown all day, made winter seem close at hand, though the month was only September. The two boys had no more than they stood up in, cotton shirts and worn jeans; Robert, the elder, shivered, thinking of the long distance they had walked, the long distance that still lay ahead of them. They were in the Black Mountains now (the Severn bridge being down, they had been obliged to go a long way around); they still had to get to the coast, Tenby, another fifty miles at least. Days and days, probably, at the rate they were going, obliged to skirt carefully around every hazard.

Chris, the younger boy, had begun to cry. He did this periodically, silently, trying not to let it show, licking in the tears as they ran down his hollow cheeks. His thin chest heaved painfully as he walked. Robert glanced at him with justifiable irritation.

"Oh, for heaven's sake, Chris! Do stop it!"

"Sorry." Chris hunched his shoulders, drew in a great sigh, and after a moment or two said humbly, as he always did, "It's just—when I think of the way I promised Mom I'd look after her. 'If anything should happen to us, you'll stay with Jenny, won't you?' she said, and I said, 'Of course I will, Mom—'"

"Yeah, yeah." Robert did not try to conceal his impatience. He had heard this a dozen times already on the way from London. An orphan himself, brought up at long range by a rich invalid grandmother, he did not set much store by family ties. He said, "For the twentieth time—Jenny will be *all right.*

Life of Riley, probably. They're okay to kids; you know they are."

"I keep hearing her *voice*," Chris said wretchedly. "All the way to the balloon she was screaming, 'Mommy! Mommy!' and 'Chris!'—I can't get it out of my mind."

What about *my* mind? Robert thought sourly. She wasn't *my* younger sister.

No use saying anything, though. Chris would shut up for an hour or so, then out it would all come again. He couldn't help it. And it wouldn't do to quarrel, Chris knew these parts. Used to come here for vacations when he was a kid.

They had been threading a narrow valley, following the windings of its shallow river. Now they were beginning to climb. Above them, government-planted coniferous forest, almost impenetrably thick, hugged the sides of the hills like dark green fur.

"Quiet!" said Robert suddenly. "What was that?"

Both boys froze like gundogs, listening.

After a considerable pause, Robert again said, "Okay. I reckon it was just dead leaves rustling."

"Sure?"

He nodded, and they started off again. Robert walked with a slight limp; every now and then he had to say, "Hey, cool it a bit, will you?" and Chris would say, "Sorry," and slow down, but he always forgot after a while and began to walk faster again.

The silence was almost complete. No traffic passed along the narrow cart track chosen by the boys. Once or twice they made long detours to avoid passing close to isolated farmhouses. Once, coming unexpectedly on a rusting tractor, stationary in a gateway, they panicked, and bolted into a close-grown, spiky larchwood, batting through the dense undergrowth to emerge, scratched and bleeding, half an hour later, in a subsidiary arm of their valley, where a tiny waterfall bounced down a boggy hill.

"Now I'm not sure where we are," said Chris, squinting at the sky. "I wish the sun would come out."

He pulled a bit of foam rubber from his pocket. It was wrapped around a tiny chrome compass that could have come from Woolworth's.

"Boy Scout," muttered Robert, but, in spite of himself, he was impressed by his companion's ability to steer a course through this wild country. "All the same," he added, "it's pretty damn crazy to carry that around—"

"Oh, what's the odds? The pins in my ears would be enough —or your leg—if they were close enough to—"

"Under skin it takes longer. They say—"

"I wouldn't want to chance finding out—"

"*Shut up!*" hissed Robert suddenly. With unexpected strength, he grabbed Chris by the arm and ran, yanking them both into the shelter of the trees.

Now the sound was unmistakable, even to Chris, whose hearing was not so good as Robert's. A small two-engined plane was cruising somewhere not far off. Presently, from in among the drooping spruce tassels, they could see it flying up the valley, could follow its somewhat erratic course as it veered from side to side. The engine was sputtering uncertainly, the wings tilted.

"Christ!" breathed Robert. "Who could possibly have—"

"Where could they have found a *plane?* I'd have thought—"

"D'you think someone had the same idea as us? The fools—"

"In a *plane?* Surely they wouldn't be so stupid—"

"Ah, listen—"

The sputter of the engine stopped; silence occupied the valley. The plane was out of sight now, around a fold of wooded hill. Then came a thunderous crash, making the ground jump under their feet. An extraordinary noise of rending, splitting trees followed, as if torn branches were coming down in sequence; the birds cried out in protest; then silence again.

The two boys looked at each other.

"What do you think?" said Chris, sweating.

"Coachmen on board. Obviously. Bloody mad to take off. Let's get away from here—"

A loud screaming began; was abruptly cut off.

"Oh—" Chris began to move in the direction of the crash. "I can't—"

Robert grabbed his arm.

"Are you absolutely off your *nut*? This isn't our—"

He began to pull Chris in the other direction. After about fifty yards they came out, unexpectedly, into a firebreak—a great open glade cutting across the woodland. Thudding footsteps made them glance uphill. A man was running down toward them. He wore the breeches and jacket of a forest ranger, but very old and weathered. He was old and weathered himself. He carried a shotgun. A dog, a thin, watchful collie, raced close at his heels. Both boys were startled almost out of their wits at the sight of him, and especially his gun, but he was thinking only of the plane.

"Come on," he panted. "This way, it was." Sensing their doubt and reluctance, he said sharply, "We may be able to do *something*."

"Fat chance—" Robert began, but the ranger snapped out, "Can't see till we get there, can we? Come *on*."

Chris went with him willingly enough; Robert scowled but followed. As they ran along the glade, he said to the man, "Why do you carry a gun? You must be barmy!"

"Always carry a gun, boy." The forester seemed surprised. "Keeping down vermin's part of the job."

"But—even in these woods—if they got a scent of it—you'd be done for. Honestly—throw it away for Pete's sake!"

"Don't be a fool," said the man shortly, and then, staring forward, "Cripes!"

They came around a curve and saw the aircraft in front of them. What was left of it. The gas tank must have exploded in midair, probably on impact with the upper branches; it was clear that the plane must have been in flames by the time it hit the ground. Now a solid pillar of fire rose, incandescent, tree high. Chris could not help a shudder of relief. Nothing in there could have survived, surely? No human at least. There was no help they could have given.

"Poor devils. They went quick enough," the man muttered, looking at the wreathed column of flame. "Lucky they crashed in the break—" thinking of his forest. "Not likely to start a forest fire. Too damp, anyway. It's a puzzle, though; what made them crash? I was looking down from the ridge—saw them tacking from side to side—as if the pilot was drunk—"

"Coachmen on board more likely." Robert gave a shiver. "Let's get away from here," he urged Chris in an undertone. And then—"Oh, *Christ*. Look at that."

Contrary to all reason, something was working its way out of the torrid combusting pyre which was all that remained of the small craft.

"God be good to us—what's *that?*" The forester stared unbelievingly at the red-hot thing that rose and writhed and sank and rose again. It was about three feet long, thick as a car tire.

"It can smell your gun," Chris found voice enough to say. "For heaven's sake—as you've *got* the gun—shoot it!"

Robert echoed urgently, "*Shoot* it—hurry up, you fool—or it'll be too late—it'll start calling the others!"

"But what *is* it?" The man's hands were shaking so much that the gun barrel drooped to the ground. The dog, subdued at the sight of the burning plane, now burst into hysterical barking.

Furiously, Robert snatched the shotgun from the man and took aim. The tubelike thing, farther from the fire now, crept and rose and swayed, gradually losing its first incandescence, taking on a pale grayish color.

"It's a coachman, of course. Haven't you ever *seen* one?" Chris asked incredulously.

The thing was now reared up on a kind of stubby platform at its rear end. It seemed to be casting about blindly with its blunt, rounded front end. Swaying, the blunt head turned in Robert's direction, just as he discharged both barrels. Blasted at fifteen-foot range, it flew into grayish fragments, which floated down like ash.

"One thing—they sure melt down quickly." Robert wiped the sweat from his forehead. "Here—take your bloody gun. Though if I were you I'd drop it in the river. Sooner or later they'll be certain to get you—you can't shoot them all."

"But what in hell *was* it?" The forester suddenly looked like an old man; under its weathering, his face was drawn and haggard as he stared at the two boys. "Was it a spook?"

"No, a coachman." And, as he continued to look blank, Robert said disbelievingly, "You don't mean to say you haven't *heard* of them?"

"I been in the woods for a matter of six weeks," he said, defensive. "Lot to do at this time of year. Don't bother with papers, much, or news." And he stooped to pat the dog huddled against his leg.

"You haven't heard of the Gretan invasion?"

He shook his head.

"Can you beat it?" The two boys looked at one another wonderingly.

"Man, you've got a lot to catch up on," Robert said. "We've been taken over. Not just England: the world. London's flat. So's Paris—Rome—Manchester—you name it, it's flat."

He stared at them.

"You're not fooling? You're telling the truth?"

Their silence convinced him.

"*Gretan*, did you say? What's that?"

"A planet. Greta. They dropped down, in a lot of things like balloons, and took us over."

"*Those* creatures?" He looked in disbelief at the flaky white fragments on the burnt grass.

Robert laughed.

"The coachmen? No, no, those are just a—a by-product. Kind of pets the Gretans brought with them."

"Parasites," Chris said.

"Why do you call them coachmen? What are they?"

"Kind of caterpillars, I believe. Nearest to that, anyway. People called them coachmen because at the front end they have that black mark shaped like a coachman's three-cornered hat—They eat metal. I reckon there isn't much metal lying around on the planet Greta—the Gretans don't use it for anything. You can see why. —So the coachmen really tucked in when they came here."

"You mean—that's what—"

"That's what happened to London and Paris? Right. Just got munched up. The coachmen," said Chris steadily, "multiply rather fast. And anything made of metal—or with metal *in* it—like reinforced concrete—just goes. Oh, god—"

He put his hands over his face at the thought of some memory.

"Won't fire burn them?" said the forester.

"They don't seem to mind heat. Well—you saw. Don't like water though."

"You say London's flat?" The forester was slowly absorbing what he had heard. "Nothing left at *all?*" They shook their heads. "What about the people?"

"Well, for the people," said Robert, "it was not good. The Gretans said they were sorry—hadn't meant *that* to happen—but there was nothing to be done, really. Anyway, they aren't too impressed with our world. Didn't seem to think we'd done too well. Better just let the coachmen munch it up. Start again fresh. They'll die out, when there's nothing left to eat."

"But—"

"The Gretans did take some kids off, though," Robert said. "Evacuated them. Back to their place."

Chris bit his lip, then said, "Look, don't let's stand here. Better get on."

"Where are you going then?" the man said.

"We want to get to Caldey. The Gretans wouldn't take *us*, you see."

"Why not? You aren't very old."

"We've both got metal bits in us. I used to be deaf—I had ear operations. Got metal stapes clips in my ears. And Rob's got a metal pin in his femur where he smashed it in a motorbike accident. The Gretans were quite straightforward about it; no use taking us there, they said, we'd only get chewed up by the coachmen back at home."

"Why go to Caldey?"

"The monastery," Robert said impatiently.

Chris explained, "The monks on the island don't use metal. Only wood. I stayed with the monks once, when I was a kid. That's why I thought of them."

"But," said the ranger, who had fallen into step with them as they walked away from the glade, "will they—the coach-men—end by eating the whole *world?* After all there's metal in the ground—?"

"They only seem to go for it in its refined form. I guess that's why the Gretans don't use it." Robert added, "I really would advise you to throw away that gun. Their sense of smell—"

The ranger looked at it doubtfully. But he could not bear to relinquish it yet; his arm had cradled the stock and barrel for so many years that it seemed like a spare limb. Reloading it, he argued, "You shot *that* one with it."

"For heaven's sake! That was just *one.*"

They had climbed up to a summit where the forest stopped abruptly and bare grass began, tufted with heather, spiked with rock. As they crossed a ridge, a great view of grassy, shadowed mountains spread out before them, and below their feet, some three hundred feet down a steep slope, a triangular lake lay steel gray under the overcast sky.

"Ah," Chris said with satisfaction. "Now I see where we are. That's Llyn-y-Fan Fach—isn't it?" he asked the man, who nodded, and then said,

"Do they—the things—coachmen—do they eat people then, too?"

"Metal's what they like best," said Robert, dry. "But yes—they aren't particular. They'll eat almost anything, actually."

Chris, without speaking, turned aside and retched, miserably, into a clump of heather.

"Come on, Chris—pull yourself together," Robert urged him. "Do we want to go east of the lake, or west?"

"East," Chris said, wiping his mouth. "We're going to have to cross a lot of roads presently—east's better. We'll have to be dead careful—"

Robert glanced behind them and suddenly yelled in alarm. "Christ! *Run for it!*"

Chris looked back, stumbled, righted himself, and started at a headlong pace down the hill, shouting to the forester, "Make for the lake!"

Behind them the whole hillside seemed in motion. A dove-colored, black and yellow flecked mass of caterpillars foamed over the summit, all gliding together in one unending ripple of movement.

The three humans spread apart, bolted for the safety of the water. The dog, crying wildly, sped ahead of them.

"Throw that—*gun* away!" panted Robert. "That's what they smelled—"

The ranger did throw it behind him in the end. But he threw it too late. The gray wave flowed over it, paused a moment, breaking into component parts, heaved up slightly, then continued on its way. Two minutes later it reached the man, who could not keep up with the boys. He went down under the silent mass. One choked cry came from him, then nothing more.

The boys, meanwhile, had reached the lake and flung themselves in. Striking out frenziedly, they reached the middle without looking back. The dog was ahead of them, a black V in the water.

Then Robert, looking over his shoulder, said, "They've forgotten about us. They found that old lock machinery on the bank."

"I've got a cramp," said Chris suddenly.

"Come on, Chris—you can do it! Turn on your back. Right, I've got you."

Swimming strongly, Robert towed the younger boy to the far side. Before climbing out, they stood for a long time, shivering, in the shallow water, scanning the hills on both sides for signs of life.

Robert said, "There must have been eggs in the plane. They must have hatched out." Chris nodded.

"Come on," Robert said at length, and they went on. The dog, whimpering, accompanied them. Robert would have driven it off with stones, but Chris said,

"Don't. He *knows* now. And his ears are better than ours."

Four days later, at dusk, they reached Giltar Point. The route to the coast had been studded with hazards—roads, garages, even telegraph poles were a source of danger. And the coast itself was a problem—lined with trailer parks, abandoned cars, mesh litter baskets full of Coke cans and foil wrappers. They had been driven farther and farther west, miles out of their way, and were then obliged to work painfully back along the rocky beaches, sometimes taking to the water, swimming round headlands. Chris, not a strong swimmer, and now, anyway, exhausted and half-starved, had been lucky enough to find a rubber tire, otherwise he would never have made it.

"That's Caldey," he said, pointing.

He was so tired that he could feel only the faintest sense of achievement at having successfully brought them so far. Besides—how could they tell? Perhaps the island had been overtaken by the same fate as the rest of the country. Horrible doubts began to attack him as he stared at the misty hump of land, just visible across the gray water. After all—eggs could be carried on a boat—or a plane could have crashed, like the one in the wood—

But as they stood shivering on the beach, one tiny light twinkled out there, like a candle floating on the sea.

"We'd better not try swimming in the dark," Robert said.

"We'd lose each other. What are the currents like here, do you know?"

"Bad, probably. I dunno. I only did it by boat."

"How far?"

"About a mile, maybe."

"Better wait till daylight."

It was hard to sleep, they were so keyed up. And it was cold. Chris managed to get himself off, at last, by his usual specific—Coleridge's *Ancient Mariner*, which he knew most of the way through. Clasping the wet, scared dog which had huddled against him for company, he murmured,

> "The moving Moon went up the sky,
>   And nowhere did abide:
> Softly she was going up,
>   And a star or two beside—"

What came after that? What was it? Oh, yes, the bit about the water snakes:

> "They moved in tracks of shining white,
>   And when they reared, the elfish light
> Fell off in hoary flakes. . . ."

Suddenly he was wide awake, and the dog was screaming. Robert was shouting.

"Get in the sea, Chris, *get in the sea!*"

He was on his feet, swaying. Daylight had come—of a sort—and now he could see what they had missed in the dark, an old rusting hulk, part of a tanker, up above the tidemark, where it had been dragged, or hurled in a winter gale. And from it a smooth stream of gray was flowing, had engulfed Robert—

Chris ran, gasping. They were at his heels, as he splashed into the waves—one of them actually reached forward to seize him, then reared back in disgust at the salt water. Now they were lined up in frustration, along the water's edge, a hideous black and gray fringe, waving from side to side, bobbing their heads. Robert was not to be seen. He was buried under an eager, seething pile, three feet deep.

Choking, weeping, Chris turned and struck out to sea, the dog beside him. Tears and salt water blinded his eyes; he could not even be sure he was going in the right direction. He had lost his tire. Would the monks see him? Would they put out a boat?

How would he ever make the crossing without Robert?

It was a long way to swim.

Who Goes Down This Dark Road?

It seems singular, remembering that first interview with Mrs. King, to think that I had no kind of premonition or foreknowledge—and yet how could I have had? If I had known, or guessed, that my intervention would result in my being brought here—would end in this tedious incarceration—I might have let well enough alone. But I did not.

Amanda King had not made any particular impression on me, save as a very *good* little girl. Among the children in the beginners' group she was not distinguished for brightness at her lessons, nor for liveliness in class; she did not have that spontaneous vivacity and wit that some small children possess, nor was she in any way remarkable when the children played games, or sang songs, or acted plays, or told stories. And yet, by the time Mrs. King came to see me, I was aware of Amanda as a particularly stable and pleasant member of the group. *Stable* seems an odd term to apply to a six year old, yet stability seemed to be Amanda's paramount quality. She was always punctual, polite, and friendly; indeed she had charming manners. I had at first assumed that it was Mrs. King who prompted the daily—and very tastefully arranged—posies, sometimes from the Kings' garden, sometimes wild flowers; but by degrees I realized that this was Amanda's own idea. Her appearance was in no way striking, yet there was something neat and attractive about her: her dark blue school pinafore and white blouse were always clean and crisp, her fair hair shining, beautifully brushed, and neatly braided, her big gray eyes serious and attentive to what was going on. She seemed a model pupil, and, though she never came first in any subject apart from spelling and deportment, seemed unlikely ever to cause either parents or teachers the slightest worry.

It was, therefore, a considerable surprise when Mrs. King came to see me, visibly distressed, one afternoon after school when I was setting up the model Saxon village for next day's intermediate class.

"Oh Mr. Thorneycroft, I'm ever so sorry to trouble you when I know how hard you work for the children, but me and Mr. King are that worried about Amanda, we don't know what to do for the best."

"About *Amanda?*" I was really amazed. "But she's the best little girl in the school."

"I know, sir, and so she's always been at home, but just lately something's got into her, something—well, peculiar. She's turned that obstinate, sir, I can't give you any idea!"

"Well, even the best children go through awkward phases," I began vaguely and consolingly. "What form does it take with Amanda, Mrs. King?"

"Sir, it's to do with her hair."

"Her hair?"

Then it did occur to me that for the last week or two, Amanda's hair had not been so shiningly neat and symmetrically braided as hitherto. And indeed that very morning, I now recalled, Amanda had turned up with the two corn-blond plaits shorn off and her hair hanging loose and rather short about her small serious face. I had made some remark on it, and she had said, "Mom thought it would be easier to keep neat if it was short."

The child next to her, Lily Thatcher, called out, "You oughter sleep with the braids under your pillow, Mandy, then you'll dream about the fellow you're going to marry!" which raised a laugh, but Amanda, rather oddly, I now recalled, said that she had buried the braids in the garden.

"What about her hair, then, Mrs. King?"

"Well, sir—I don't know how to put it so you won't think either I or the child is crazy—" I noticed with astonishment that the placid-seeming Mrs. King had tears in her eyes—"but she's got this notion that there's people living in her hair."

Various possibilities flashed through my mind. I said delicately, "You're quite sure, Mrs. King, that it's not a simple case of nits, head parasites—something like that?"

"Sir! How could you think such a thing? There's some families in the village I wouldn't put it past them, but my Amanda's always been perfectly clean—I've washed her hair myself every Saturday night since she was born."

"I must say her hair always does look beautifully clean," I said quickly. "Well, if that is the case, you don't think it's possible that she *imagines* she has something of the sort? Children sometimes have such odd private worries—"

"No, sir, no, it's not like that. No, it's *people* she says are living on top of her head. In among the hair, like. She says—" Mrs. King faltered, "she said the hair seems like a forest to them."

"She's playing a game with you, Mrs. King," I suggested. "It's just a piece of pretense. I remember when I was a boy I had an imaginary bear—oh, I carried him around with me for years!"

"A game it may be, sir, but it's dead serious to her," Mrs. King said worriedly. "Every day I have the very deuce of the job, you'll pardon me, sir, to get her hair brushed. 'Don't *do* that, Mom, you'll drive them out of the forest,' she says, and she screams and screams; it makes my Joe really wild; he's threatened to give her a good hiding if she won't be more reasonable. And lately, sir—oh, I've begun to wonder if she's going mental." Mrs. King here fairly burst out crying. "She talks such rubbish, sir! All about chariots and temples and sacred stones and armies and navies—it's not right, sir, it really isn't. And sometimes what she says doesn't make sense at all; it's not proper language; you can't make head or tail of it, and she'll go on like that for hours."

"Did you mention this to Dr. Button?"

"Well, I did, sir—I didn't take Amanda to the office for fear of scaring her. I just told him, and he fairly snapped my head off and said she was a perfectly healthy child and not to fuss him with a bit of kid's moonshine."

This sounded true to form. I said cautiously, "Well, what did you want me to do, Mrs. King?"

"Oh, sir, if you could just *talk* to Amanda about it a bit! She thinks the world of you, sir; if you could just reason this nonsense out of her head—"

"Very aptly put, Mrs. King."

She looked at me rather blankly, so I promised that I would see what I could do. "Supposing I take Amanda for a walk, Mrs. King, tomorrow, after school—I could ask her to show me where she picks her delightful bunches of flowers. Then it won't seem too like a formal interview."

"Oh, Mr. Thorneycroft, I don't know how to thank you—"

I pointed out that I hadn't done anything yet, but she went away evidently relieved to have pushed the responsibility onto somebody else, even if only temporarily.

Next afternoon Amanda agreed, with grave politeness, to take me across the Common and show me where she picked her cowslips and ladies' smocks. I thought there was no sense in deferring the question, so as soon as we were away from the village, I said, "Your mother asked me to talk to you, Amanda, about this idea you have that—er, that people are living in your hair."

She looked up at me calmly, with a surprisingly adult expression in her gray eyes, and said, "Yes, I thought perhaps she had."

I said, gently, not wanting to seem unsympathetic or mocking, "What sort of people are they, Amanda?"

She answered at once. "They're a tribe of Gauls, the Veneti.

They were defeated, you see, by the Romans, in a big sea battle, and driven out of their homes. They built a new town, but
then it was destroyed—it sank in the sea. And so they collected
up what they could of their belongings—and now they live in
my hair. It's like a forest to them, you see."

I was startled, to say the least.

"But Amanda—how did you come to know about the
Veneti?"

"I can hear them," she said matter-of-factly. "Talking.
Through my skull."

"But they were a long time ago! More than two thousand
years."

"I suppose they got through it fast, somehow. Some people
go quicker than others."

I said, "How could they all get onto your head, though?
They were full-size people—a whole tribe of them. How could
they all camp on one little corn-colored nut?"

She gave me a look as closely approaching to impatience as
natural politeness would permit.

"Things seem a different size, don't you see, when they're in
different places. If I saw you a long way off—you'd look small,
wouldn't you? Or if I saw you beside a *huge* monster." Her
eyes widened, and I remembered that, after all, she was still
only a six year old. The word *relative* was probably outside her
vocabulary.

"What sort of language do they talk, these people,
Amanda?" This fable she had spun for herself was wonder-
fully coherent so far; I wondered where she read or heard of
the Veneti, who, I recalled, had been vanquished by Caesar in
Brittany.

"Well, they talk two languages," she told me.

"Can you remember any of the words?"

She reeled of a string of jargon which was meaningless to
me, full of X sounds and CH sounds; I became more and more
interested remembering medical cases of glossolalia, "speaking
with tongues," which sometimes occur in religious fanatics or

mental patients—but in an otherwise matter-of-fact little girl of six?

"And what is the other language?"

She then started me out of my wits by replying, "Una salus victis nullam sperare salutem" (there is but one safe thing for the vanquished: not to hope for safety).

"Good heavens, Amanda! Where did you hear that?"

"One of them up there said it." She pointed to her flaxen locks.

"Can you remember any more?"

"Quid nunc it per iter tenebricosum—"

"Illuc," I said it with her, "unde negant redire quemquam."

"You know that too?" she said, turning the gray eyes on me.

"I have heard it, yes. What was the people's town called, Amanda—the town that sank in the sea?"

"It was called Is."

"Do you know the names of the gods they worship?"

"They must not be spoken or written down. There is a serpent's egg that must be thrown into the air."

"And caught in a white cloak?"

"Yes. But just now their holy men are very worried," she said, turning to me, frowning—she looked absurdly like her mother.

"Why are they worried, Amanda?"

"They have signs from—from the ones who can tell the future—that there is going to be another very bad happening—and they are going to have to move again, their circle of sacred stones and all the people with their things. Oh!" she cried, clasping her hands to her fair head. "I do *hope* Mom isn't going to cut off all my hair! She said she might do that! Please tell her not to, Mr. Thorneycroft!"

"All right, Amanda—don't worry. I'll tell her."

"Look," she said, cheering up, "this is where the cowslips grow."

We both picked a bunch and started for home. I was very silent and thoughtful, but Amanda, having had my promise about the hair-cutting, skipped along beside me quite light-heartedly with her bunch of cowslips, humming in a tuneless but not unpleasant little voice.

I, needless to say, was wondering what to do, and hardly looked where I was going. Which is why I didn't hear the car till it was right behind us.

It was young, feckless Colin Gaddock, who works in the gas station over at Maynard's Cross; he always comes home at a crazy pace, hell-bent on getting to his evening's enjoyment. His side mirror caught the child's jacket as he shot past us, and she was dragged, shrieking, five hundred yards up the road before he could brake to a stop.

He's doing time for manslaughter now; I'd like to think it had taught him a lesson, but fear that he's the kind of hopeless lout who will presently come out of jail and do exactly the same thing again.

I could never go into a butcher's shop again. The sight of a piece of steak. . . .

People said I'd had a breakdown, and everyone was very sorry for me. But actually it's simpler than that. What happened was, that the Veneti transferred from Amanda's head to mine.

And I'm a bit bothered, now, because their Druids are predicting another catastrophe.

Power Cut

The wind, like a flapping blanket, beat and thrashed and swung and slapped and buffeted, making each casement rattle, every door sway and creak. The wind sighed in the chimney, clanked in the pipes, and gibbered in the TV aerial. Rain slammed on to the slates and dashed in cascades against the stuttering windows. The cottage was massively built; its two-foot-thick rock walls were solidly planted on a Cornish hillside. It bore with indifference the lash of the gale. But all the air inside it was disturbed, full of pockets and sudden eddies; in spite of closed doors and shuttered windows, the weather seemed to pass right through the house, as if, Thomas felt, it were only a skeleton house, a diagram of a building. He put out his hand to feel the wall. It felt thick, immovable, though chill and sweating with damp; but as soon as he removed his hand, the fluttering air suggested to him again that he was standing in the middle of the moor.

Or in the middle of nowhere.

He called, "Celia? Where are you?"

Her voice came from above. "I'm upstairs. Switching on all the heaters. Airing the blankets. Everything feels horribly damp. Why blasted old Mrs. Tredinnick couldn't come as I asked her to and switch on the radiators. . . . Can you turn on the fan heater in the living room?"

"Okay."

He felt his way along the side of the kitchen, navigating by the feel of the smooth, square metal shapes. Refrigerator, oven, washing machine, dryer, dishwasher, two steel sinks (with a garbage disposal unit in one), electric furnace, then a cupboard. Then came the door into the living room. From twenty years of living in it, he knew their London house intimately, so that he had no need to feel his way, could walk freely from room to room. But the cottage was strange territory nowadays; he had not set foot in it for seven or eight years. Had not wanted to.

It had been a happy retreat when they first bought it—bare and primitive though it had been. It was surrounded by grass and heather, a place to come for weekends and holidays with the children, where they half-camped, cooking sausages on sticks over peat fires. Those times were far in the past. They had swum in the old quarry, which the children nicknamed The Bottomless Pool (the children wearing lifejackets at all times in case of cramp from the nerve-chilling cold of the water); they had fished in the stream and taken immense walks on the moor.

Then, later, the cottage had become a refuge. They had come on escape-weekends, fleeing from those same children, grown large now, and defiant, inhabiting the London house with their friends like advance occupying forces from a hostile planet. During that period they had taken pains (or Celia had —he had little interest in the process) to render the cottage more comfortable, putting in electricity with all its benefits: radio, TV, a deepfreeze so there was always food in store, more furniture, carpets, and color schemes. Celia's friend the interior decorator Gerard Barron had contributed the color schemes. And the result of that was an article, with pictures, in one of the color supplements.

Then there had been a period when Celia came for weekends on her own, or with Gerard Barron.

Then there had been the period when, theoretically, the cottage had been ceded to their eldest son, Simon. In theory Simon had paid rent for it. That period had lasted for an uneasy three or four years, punctuated with battles:

"When did that boy last pay you any rent? Come on now—has he paid any at all this year?"

"Well—"

"Well what?"

"He did give me two of his pictures. In a gallery they'd fetch a hundred pounds at least—"

"A gallery? Hah! What gallery? Booker looked at some of them and told me they looked as if they'd been done by a demented four year old. That rent has got to be paid in *cash*—or he has to clear out—he and those friends of his! God knows what goes on in that place."

Then Celia, returning from a weekend in Looe (with whom, he had not inquired; not with Gerard Barron, that was long finished) had called at the cottage and found nobody there. "But the *mess*, Thomas! I was really appalled! All our beautiful color schemes covered with crazy murals. Mud and cigarette ends all over the carpets. They're absolutely ruined. Dirt everywhere. The windows painted silver so you can't see out. The furniture half scraped—that valuable rosewood table! I could have burst out crying. I've *never* been so upset in my whole *life*."

Simon had been equally angry.

"But you *gave* me the cottage! You said it was mine, that I could do what I liked with it."

"Not to wreck our expensive furniture. Not to turn the whole place into a disgusting shambles. Eating off the floor! Leaving the dishwasher open to rust—smashing the TV screen!"

"That's the way I and my friends *like* to live—we can do without all your ridiculous pampering luxury, your endless gadgets. Even an answering device on the phone—in the middle of Bodmin Moor, for Christ's sake!"

After this, Simon had been told to get out of the cottage, and after some more dispute, he had left, saying to his mother that he would never forgive her; for tax reasons, the cottage was said to belong to Celia.

She had had the place redecorated and tidied up, but this time her heart was not in it.

After that, for a period of several years, it had been used less and less.

And then, and then. . . .

He had switched on the fan heater in the living room, which smelled depressingly of mildew, and then returned to the kitchen. Here the chimney was blocked; the howl of the gale was less audible.

"Anything you'd like me to do?" he called up the stairs.

"No . . . no," Celia's voice came down impatiently. "Well —yes; switch on the electric stove—that'll help dry the place out."

He felt his way to the stove and located the switch. After a moment, holding his hands a few inches above the top of the stove, he could feel the plates begin to glow.

They were here to try and mend their marriage, a hopeless project, perhaps. The weather certainly wasn't helping, terrible for early June. They were here to recover from Simon's death. And their own feelings towards each other about it. They were here to tidy and clear out the cottage so that it could be sold. They were here to bury Simon's memory.

"I won't have that boy in the house another *day*, I tell you."

"But Thomas—he's been so ill. He looks so terrible. If you could only see him—"

That had been a tactical error on Celia's part.

"I don't need to see him, thank you. I can smell him—when he's been smoking that stuff. *And* hear him. If he puts that bloody record on once more—'Gimme, gimme, gimme all you pro-o-o-mised me!' "

Then the police had come round. A pound of cannabis had been found in Simon's room.

"No, I am not going to pay his bail. Let him stew in his own juice. I wash my hands of him. If you hadn't spoiled him rotten—given him all he ever asked for—"

"Oh, you're just a cold-hearted, vindictive bastard—I truly believe you still hold it against him—after all these years—over twenty years now—"

Twenty years of not being able to see. Did she think that the length of time reduced the sense of loss? Twenty years since he had been able to look at the black and blue stormy sky which he had to imagine careering past overhead; the patches of steel-and-amber-colored light and the rain squalls chasing each other over the moor.

"For heaven's sake, he was only a tiny boy then, four years old—He didn't know what he was doing—"

A spoiled, strong, tyrannical four year old with a grievance and an aerosol can of oven spray.

There came a loud, sharp knock at the back door. Even above the wail and gibber of the wind he could hear its peremptory summons—bang-bang—and a pause—bang-bang again.

"Celia!" he called. "There's someone at the back door."

"Well, answer it, then! Don't be so bloody helpless," she called impatiently. "I'm in the middle of making up the beds."

He felt his way out of the kitchen, along the narrow slate-floored back passage, where the original granite of the cottage could still be felt. And smelled. He fumbled past coats hanging on hooks. The back door was still locked. He turned the key, pressing both hands to move it in its rusty socket, and opened the door. A gust of rain slapped him in the face, as if the weather were seizing the chance to take more tangible possession of the cottage.

"Yes?" he said. "Hello—who is it?" He had caught Celia's impatience. "Who is there?"

He recognized the cracked old voice, though he had not heard it recently.

"It's Anna Tredinnick, Mr. Michaels. I came to ask about my cat."

"Oh, good evening, Mrs. Tredinnick. Why—"

Why the hell didn't you turn on the radiators, as my wife

wrote and asked you to, he felt like saying, but then thought better. No sense in antagonizing the old girl, who was their nearest neighbor, the only caretaker they had been able to secure. He amended his question to, "Why don't you come in?"

"No," she said. "I won't do that. I'm all wet—I'm all wet," she repeated, in her sing-song west-country voice. "Just feel how wet I am, Mr. Michaels." And she took his hand before he could prevent her and guided it over what felt like the stiff wrinkles of some sodden, felted-up material. He removed his hand with fastidious speed as soon as he could withdraw it from her cold, skinny old claw.

"Well—" he said irritably. What was that about her cat?

"Your cat, Mrs. Tredinnick? What about your cat?"

"The young 'un. Simon. When he was here. He had the old puss up to the cottage. He was always mortal fond o' cats, young Simon."

"*Simon* had it here? But we told you, Mrs. Tredinnick, that you were on *no* account to let him have the key—on no account to let him *into* the cottage. We told you he wasn't to be allowed to use it any more, after what he and his friends did before." (Besides—*when* was he at the cottage?)

"Ah, I told him that, Mr. Michaels. 'You bean't allowed to go in there, no more,' I told him. 'You better go off somewhere else, afore I call the police, like Mr. Michaels says I got to.' 'You mind your blurry business, you old hag,' he says to me. Proper rude, he was. He didn't take no notice o' me. He had his own key, see? *I* couldn't stop him. And the pussy was up here, too. The old puss always did go up, if ever young Simon was there. So then I did call the police, and Sergeant Pollard from Bodmin, he come out—and I give him my key to the place—but young Simon he were gone by then. Likely he just come to fetch summat he left behind. But since then the old puss he haven't been back home; no, I haven't seen him since that day."

"Well I'm very sorry, Mrs. Tredinnick, but there's no cat

here. You're welcome to come in and look around if you want—"

Just the same, he very much hoped that the old thing wouldn't; she smelt perfectly disgusting, of wet, muddy, dirty wool and damp, unwashed old age.

"If your cat had been shut up in here, it would surely have run out as soon as we opened up the house—"

No, though; it might not have, he thought, gagging a little, on the stench of wet old woman and the thought that just then occurred to him.

"Ah—how long ago *was* this, Mrs. Tredinnick? When was my son here?"

For it was now five weeks since Simon, released from his eighteen-month term, had been found burned to death in somebody's barn, together with the barn itself, and most of the hay it contained. Careless smoking, was the verdict. Death by misadventure. Simon must have come to the cottage shortly before? To collect some cache he had left here? Or hoping to stay, after being turned ruthlessly away from the London house?

"No, Simon. This isn't your home any more. I'm sorry."

He had not been sorry. He had been immensely relieved.

But if the cat had been shut in the cottage five weeks, it could not have survived.

"Celia?" he called nervously up the stairs. "Mrs. Tredinnick's here, asking about her cat. You—you haven't seen a cat anywhere?"

"What? I can't hear you."

He walked to the foot of the stairs and repeated his question. After a moment or two Celia came running down.

"For God's sake, shut that back door!" she snapped. "Half the Atlantic's blowing into the house—there's a lake in the back passage already!"

Impatiently she pushed past him and slammed the rattling door.

"But Mrs. Tredinnick's out there!"

"No she isn't. There was nobody outside."

"Are you sure?"

"Positive."

"Oh well," he said, "I suppose the old girl must have gone off again as soon as she was certain the cat wasn't here. I suppose you *haven't* seen a cat anywhere? She sounded a bit distraught about it. I hope it's not shut in somewhere." He sniffed. "I can't stand the smell."

"Thomas." Celia's voice, too, sounded strange, he noticed.

"Yes, what?"

"Simon must have been here. Before—before. His bed had been slept in. He must have spent a night here."

"Yes," he said. "The old girl just said so. Simon must have had a key we didn't know about. But she called the police, and by the time they turned up, he had left."

"Oh, god, oh *god!*" From the sound, he could tell that Celia must have sat by the kitchen table and laid her head on her arms. "Poor wretched boy— Hounded about—from place to place—as if he were some kind of *monster*— Ending up in that barn—"

"*He was* some kind of monster," Thomas said coldly. "He had completely abandoned the rules of civilized behavior."

"How could you just *abandon* your own *child?*"

"Shut up, Celia! We've been through all this—over and over. There's no sense in having it all again. Get a grip on yourself, for god's sake. Here we are, out in the middle of the moor, in the middle of a bloody tempest—this just isn't the time for hysterics."

"I can't think why we came here," she said abruptly. The chair scraped, her voice shifted; she had stood up. "It's hopeless. This place is haunted. It was crazy to come—"

"We had to come sometime," he pointed out reasonably. "If we're going to sell the place, we've got to tidy it and find out what's here. Come on—pull yourself together. You'll solve no problems by running away."

"Running away? Isn't that what you've been doing all

along?" she said furiously. "Running away from the problems of our own— *Oh!*"

"What's up *now?*" he said, for her last exclamation seemed to have no connection with the preceding words.

"All the lights have gone out. Power failure I suppose. The gale must have blown down a cable somewhere—That's *really* torn it. We can't stay in this place if nothing's working."

"Why? It probably won't last long. We can burn candles. I expect there's still some peat in the shed."

"Don't be stupid! We'd freeze! Everything's sopping. Besides, we can't cook, or heat the water—or even *get* any water if the electric pump's not working—"

A drawer rattled; she appeared to be hunting for candles. She said, and he could hear panic in her voice, "My god, it's so *dark!* I'd forgotten how pitch dark it is out here on the moor."

Now you know how dark it is where I am, he thought.

"There don't seem to be any candles. Simon must have used them all."

Took them to set fire to the hay in that barn? he wondered.

"I'll phone Mrs. Tredinnick and see if she has any."

But the phone in the living room was dead, too, when he tried it. Presumably the gale had cut out the telephone, as well as the power lines. Replacing the receiver, he knocked his elbow, as he remembered doing so many times in the past on the shelf that held the recorded-message gadget. Swearing absently, he rubbed his arm. In doing so, he must accidentally have switched on the machine, for his own voice suddenly spoke out, loud and harsh, just above his right ear.

"Simon: listen. Simon. This is just to tell you that, if by any chance, you should turn up at the cottage, Mrs. Tredinnick has our instructions to call the police. You are not—repeat, *not* —to use the cottage. Is that understood?"

Amplified to twice its volume, his voice sounded harsh, but also nervous; there seemed to be a note of crazy pleading in its threat.

By contrast, the voice of his son was merely mocking.

"Hello, Dad, dear Daddy? By the time you get this, I'll be gone-o—so you'll be able to enjoy the pleasures of the place all on your own. All on your loney-own, won't that be nice for you, Daddy? You can use the polisher, the blender, the vacuum cleaner, the dishwasher, the garbage-destructor—you'd better use *that*, Daddy, that'll be just what you need—you can watch the TV, you can listen to the radio, even, as a special treat, listen to some of my records. *Won't* that be fun? You can cook yourself some scrumptious frozen lasagna, and cuddle up in bed with your electric blanket. But, before you have supper, if I were you, I'd look in the dishwasher, Daddy, because old Mrs. Busy Tredinnick may be wanting her cat and it might have got in there. You know how cats are, Daddy. Right? Right. So long, then. Love from Simon."

The tape ran to its end and began to squeal. Then it cut out.

I can't really have heard that, he thought, after a moment. I must have imagined it.

It can't have been switched on, because the power is off.

He tried the telephone. It was still dead. Feeling his way back to the kitchen, he called:

"Celia. Hey, Celia?"

"What?" Her voice came from the coatrack near the back door. It was muffled, as if she were putting on a hood.

"Is the power still off?"

"Yes, it is. I'm going down to Mrs. Tredinnick to borrow some candles."

"Walking?"

"In this weather? Are you kidding? No, I'm taking the car. If she hasn't any, I'll knock up the shop."

"You'll come back?" He despised the pleading in his own voice.

"Yes." But did she mean it? He was not sure.

The front door slammed. Instantly after its bang he heard another noise: the howl of a cat, the loud, resonant, desperate wauling cry of a cat that has been shut up in a box or basket and is frantic to get out. The whole house seemed to reverberate with its meowing.

Thomas hated cats—couldn't stand them anywhere near him or in the house at all. Early on, *that* had had to be made plain to the children, who had, at times, begged for kittens, offered by ignorant neighbors. Once, Simon had actually brought one home; it had had to be taken back to its place of origin.

Thomas went to the front door and opened it, shouting, "Celia. Celia! Just a minute. That bloody old woman's cat *is* in here somewhere. Come back!"

But the sound of the car's engine was his only answer, just audible above the roar of the wind.

He went back to the kitchen. And now the cat's frenzied yelling seemed to be coming from one distinct point. Groping his way past refrigerator, stove (now gone stone-cold again), Laundrymaster, spin dryer, he came to the dishwasher, which seemed to be vibrating from the urgency to be free of the creature trapped inside it. Lucky nobody switched it on, Thomas thought.

But why had the cat not cried before? And how could it have survived five weeks, shut in there?

No need to ask *who* shut it in, he thought, pulling down the hinged front panel.

He expected a furry body to shoot out past him and escape. But that was not what happened. The howling went on. Was the cat somehow tied in there, trapped?

Gingerly, with acute repugnance, Thomas extended a cautious hand in among the framework of racks which made up the interior of the machine—and then pulled back his hand with a cry of disgust and fright even louder than the yells of the trapped creature itself. He had touched a mess of cold, congealed, slimy fur and bone, which gave, horribly, under his exploring fingers.

Cursing, he jumped toward the sink and turned the tap, wishing to wash the revolting scummy slime off his fingers.

But no water came from the tap. He had to grope in a drawer for a towel and rub, rub, rub at his hands. Nothing would shift the memory of that horrible contact.

Now the whole kitchen seemed filled with the stink of wet fur and cat's urine. And now he knew what that crazy, wicked, revengeful boy meant when he said, "You'd better use the garbage-destructor, Daddy—that'll be just what you need."

How could Simon *do* such a thing? A boy who had loved cats?

In the blacked-out village Celia was knocking in vain at the door of Mrs. Tredinnick's cottage. A neighbor, passing with flashlight, told her, "You'll find nobody to home therr, midear. Hadn't you heard, then? The old lady was drowned in the pool, top o'moor, last Friday week, that black foggy night. 'Tis thought she were out a-hunting for her puss. . . ."

And in the pitch-dark cottage kitchen Thomas, standing rigid with horror, heard the voice of the wind begin to abate. But, taking its place the sounds of man-made power inside the cottage began to rise and menace. The refrigerator hummed and stuttered, the spin dryer roared, the vacuum cleaner surged, the telephone maniacally rang, the television boomed, the blender chattered, the garbage-destructor rumbled, and a record player, turned up to a shattering intensity of sound yelled:

"*Gimme*, GIMME, *GIMME* all you *PROMISED* meeee. . . ."

Thomas opened the front door and ran out, taking his own darkness with him.